ARTIFICIAL INSURRECTION

Book Three of The Terre Hoffman Chronicles

First Edition

Copyright ©2022 by Herman Steuernagel

This is a work of fiction. Names, characters, places, and incidents either are the product of the author's imagination or are used fictitiously. Any resemblance to actual persons, living or dead, events or locales is entirely coincidental.

All international rights reserved. No part of this publication may be reproduced, stored or transmitted in any form or by any means, electronic, mechanical, photocopying, recording, scanning, or otherwise without written permission from the publisher. It is illegal to copy this book, post it to a website, or distribute it by any other means whether digital or printed without permission in writing from the copyright owner.

ISBN: 978-1-990505-04-1 (paperback)

ISBN: 978-1-990505-03-4 (ebook)

Cover by MiblArt

Edited by Novel Approach Manuscript Services

https://www.hermansteuernagel.com

ARTIFICIAL INSURRECTION

HERMAN STEUERNAGEL

THE TERRE HOFFMAN CHRONICLES | BOOK THREE

Chapter One

Terre

"Are you going to get that?"

Hailey Prescott sat behind the driver's seat of their refitted gas-powered SUV. She nodded toward Terre Hoffman's crotch as the SUV and their small party wove down the highway at a snail's pace. His phone was on vibrate, but its buzz was clearly audible over the engine.

The highway was obstructed, as if the driverless cars had been intentionally arranged so that they'd be forced to slow, weave, and take as long as possible to get onto the freeway.

And Terre had no doubt that was *exactly* what had happened.

He just had no idea why.

The phone was unrelenting against his thigh, and there was only one person it could be. Only one person had access to a network separate from the public's cell phone towers and networks.

Terre didn't want to answer. He had no intention of speaking to his ex-employer again.

He had just barely evaded the destruction of the Las Vegas Strip only two hours ago. Terre tried to block out the visions threatening to shut him down before he could complete his mission: the wayward machines fleeing the city; the Sentinels firing upon any human they came across; buildings crashing down above him. It had been the third time in three months that wayward machines had attacked the place he was in.

It seriously made Terre wonder if he was just a magnet for bad luck.

Terre's hand strayed to the pendant that hung from his neck. It had been a gift from his daughter, Sarah, who had picked it out for him during a time he so desperately wanted to go back to. She'd said it was a good luck charm, which Terre supposed was *something*. He was alive, at least.

At this point, though, it was hard to tell if being alive was a blessing or a curse.

There was no longer anything meaningful for Terre to live for. It appeared his many attempts to wipe the slate clean and start again were futile. The nightmare continued, and he had no ability to wake from the deadly grip of reality.

Terre glanced at the two Canadians he had picked up along the way in the back seat. At least one of them was snoring, maybe both. Both Annika Phillips and Becky Johnson had been through enough to have earned the break. In addition to running from the homicidal bots on the Las Vegas Strip, the women had climbed over forty floors, while dehydrated, in an attempt to rescue Annika's sister, Cheyenne; only to discover the girl had been abducted by her Keeper robot, Ember. That said, despite the mayhem they'd encountered, it surprised Terre that rest for the women was at all possible with the stopping and starting needed to avoid the stalled vehicles on the highway.

We're never going to get anywhere like this, he mused.

If the streetlights had been functioning, it would have made traversing over obstacles, curbs, and parking lots a little easier, but the power still hadn't returned to the city, leaving them in near complete darkness.

Instead, red and blue flashes from non-automated police vehicles filled the gaps between buildings that were blocks away. Floodlight beams running on generators and battery-operated flashlights waved across the Strip in mockery of the light shows that would have danced along it only twenty-four hours prior. Terre could almost imagine the beam from the top of the Luxor's pyramid stretching to the clouds; a beacon signaling the oasis in the desert that was Las Vegas.

"We've been at this for two hours." Terre was desperate to delay answering his phone. "There has to be a better way through."

"If you have any bright ideas, I'm all ears. In the meantime, you can answer your goddamn phone," Hailey griped. "You might be able to ignore it, but it's driving *me* crazy. I'm trying to concentrate here."

Nothing came to mind, so Terre resigned himself to letting her do the driving.

Terre could only guess Hailey had commandeered the SUV from someone's private collection. That said, she did seem to be privy to more intel than he did, so perhaps she also had access to a repository of issued equipment. Fredricks, it seemed, had been holding back on making Terre aware of both personnel and utilities that could have been useful when ordering Terre to find the wayward programmer in the middle of the desert.

Commands from megaphones and speaker systems in the distance broke the silence the powerless city should have possessed. The words grew increasingly muffled as they increased their distance from the Strip, but Terre had heard enough. National Guard officers were issuing commands for civilians to retreat to the evacuation centers. It was obvious to Terre that since they were still making the requests, the soldiers didn't yet possess the human resources needed to enforce the rules their superiors had set into place.

Terre was hardly surprised. The authorities were likely being pulled in a hundred different directions between the bots that were still rogue and the men and women eager to take advantage of a city in chaos. Bursts of blaster fire echoed from all corners of the city, often followed by machine gun fire. The mismatch of artillery declared that the soldiers were ill-equipped to deal with the robot invasion; a fact solidified in Terre's mind that those higher in the chain of command were unwilling to admit: they had created artificial monsters.

San Francisco had fallen six weeks ago. The military failing to brief or adequately prepare soldiers to handle a second uprising was nothing short of criminal.

The world was falling apart at the seams, and yet somehow Fredricks was able to get through despite no working signal. It aggravated Terre to no end. Not even a crippled cell network could give him the reprieve he longed for. He could only imagine the signal was being rerouted directly to him via satellite.

Regardless of the method, Terre had no interest in the madness. Despite his best efforts, rogue machines had unleashed havoc in yet another city, and once again, he was in the direct path of the out-of-control machines. Terre had come to Vegas to escape; to unwind; to breathe for a damn minute. He was having a hard time mustering motivation enough to navigate through the desert to find the smart-ass engineer likely behind the latest surge in Sentinel attacks. Kristopher was supposed to be knee-deep in the jungles of South America, not making a mess at the Hoover Dam— whatever that mess might be.

Reluctantly, Terre palmed his cell and lifted it to his ear, but not before he noticed that his battery was getting dangerously low.

"You're late," Terre said. "I was expecting your call hours ago."

"What, no hello? What took you so damn long to answer?" The familiar gruff voice grated on every one of Terre's nerves. He had left the Agency for a reason. He didn't want to be involved in these missions. Fredricks continued without waiting for a reply. "And don't get smart, Hoffman. As you can imagine, we've been a little preoccupied."

Terre fought the urge to laugh. Fredricks had locked himself in a command room while Terre and his companions had been outrunning robots, terrorists, and the world crashing down on them in the most literal sense he could think of.

"That makes two of us, Fredricks. We haven't exactly been having a picnic here ourselves."

The SUV lurched as they hopped onto the sidewalk for what seemed like the hundredth time that evening as Hailey navigated their way around the latest row of stalled vehicles.

"Well, don't get the blanket out just yet, Hoffman. What's your status?"

"I hope you're going to give me some more details about exactly what I'm supposed to be doing."

Get out of the city. Find K. That was about the extent of what Fredricks had relayed during their last call.

"Glad to hear you're finally on board."

"It's not like you gave me much choice."

Fredericks's response was terse. "Duty isn't a choice, son."

Terre briefly considered the events of the day as fighter jets screamed overhead, racing toward the Strip. "I guess if you hadn't called, I'd probably be dead by now, so I suppose I owe you some thanks for that."

The orbs that had threatened to blow the city to pieces now hovered as if in stasis, their blue lights glowing but noticeably dimmed. Onyx drones like those currently dotting the skyline had launched an assault on San Francisco that had decimated the city's entire infrastructure. Given that the jets merely circled the orbs without firing, Terre knew all he needed to know about the government's priorities. Nothing had changed in their stance of "protect our assets at all costs."

"Though I imagine there will be more casualties before the day is done," Terre mused.

"I couldn't care less about saving your ass. There's far more on the line here, Hoffman. Intel believes Kristopher may have reactivated the bots. There's an unsanctioned connection to the military's network pinging from the area around the Hoover Dam, but we haven't been able to get close enough to investigate. It's piggybacking off one of the most heavily guarded networks in the country. Even our analysts can't seem to crack through whatever crazy protections Klein has set up."

There it was; the answer Terre had been waiting for all morning. But the whole scenario didn't make a whole lot of sense.

"K and I nearly got ourselves killed trying to shut these machines down," Terre remarked. "Why the hell would he want to start them back up?"

"That's what we need you for, Hoffman. Aside from these isolated attacks, the bots seem to be congregating in various locations across the country. We've traced the bots' movements and intercepted where their command nodes are receiving direction from. From the western front, all roads seem to point back to the Hoover Dam. We know Kristopher's involved, but we need you to work on the 'how and why.'"

Terre pondered a moment, recalling the day's events. "Earlier today, I saw a stream of bots headed out of the city. Do you think that might be where they were headed?"

"I'm confident it is. We're getting similar reports from all over the country. But we're in the dark as to why."

Terre cast his eyes to the back seat again, his gaze resting on the two women asleep there. "Are you hearing any word of humans being brought in?"

"No specifics. Why'd you ask?"

"I've got a woman here with me," Terre said. "We think a bot's kidnapped her sister."

"I've told you all I know. We really need a pair of eyes on the ground to give us more details."

Bullshit, Terre thought. Fredricks had easily tracked him to a Las Vegas casino, and they had intel that his former coworker was at the Hoover Dam, yet they didn't know if there was a procession of machines leading captured people headed in that direction?

There was more Fredricks wasn't filling him in on. In fact, Terre was sure Fredricks was keeping a whole multitude of sins under wraps. Namely, why Terre was the one being sent in instead of a special ops team. If the intervention was really that crucial, a network specialist wouldn't be the prime candidate for the mission.

And why had the Agency sent Hailey to babysit him?

"You really need *me* to go in?" Terre asked. "There are jets flying overhead as we speak. Why can't they do a flyby?"

"Whatever Klein's doing out there is jamming our instruments. We can see the bots are building something, but beyond that, we're blind. Between these attacks and all methods of civilian transportation being hijacked across the country, we assume he's draining power from the Dam. But we don't know why or how. Our sensors can't get a read on any of it."

Terre gave Hailey a sidelong glance. She'd suggested something similar back in the city, but Terre had brushed it off.

"So, send in someone better equipped to intercept him. I'm just a Network Analyst. I really don't understand ..."

"If *we* don't deal with this," Fredricks interrupted, "and

when I say *we*, I literally mean *you*, Hoffman, there won't be a second chance. The Agency doesn't have the time or the resources to do anything but take the kid out and ask for forgiveness later. I've had to pull a lot of strings just to get one shot at you going in and talking him down. The only thing saving his ass right now is that the two of you managed to quiet the tech down for a month and a half. Understand this, Hoffman; we're officially at war. If the top brass are notified of verified intel showing Kristopher's behind this, they won't ask questions. So far, they're happy to let me handle it, but if I don't come up with the goods, Klein's out of luck. Vegas isn't the only city under attack right now; it's all hands on deck trying to stop the Sentinels' advances."

Terre swallowed and rubbed his temple with his free hand.

At war with our own creations. No matter who wins, we lose.

"Lucky for Klein, Special Forces can't spare anyone. Intel agreed to give us a shot because I convinced them I could assign someone to talk him down. That someone is you. There is nobody else."

Terre rubbed his temple. He really had no desire to get thrown into the middle of trying to save the world yet again. But K was a good kid. If this was all Hoffman had to negotiate to keep the kid alive, what choice did he have?

"I don't like this any more than you do," Fredricks continued. "But if anyone can talk some sense into that kid, it's you."

"I don't have to tell you how I feel about having to go on your rescue mission." Terre's eye lingered on the dots hovering above them. "But if we're truly at war, why are we still unwilling to fire first? Why aren't the jets taking down the Onyx? We're still protecting dollars over lives?"

"I don't pretend to be privy to any sort of strategy, Hoffman. You might find it hard to believe, but I'm in the same situation as you. I'm a tech supervisor; none of this is part of my wheelhouse. All I can do is follow the orders assigned to me, which I expect you to do as well under the circumstances. Employed or not, you have to do this."

Terre sighed. Could he refuse? Could a civilian be subject to court-martial? He would have to brush up on his military law, but from what he remembered from his political sciences class, if the President had declared war, it was possible.

The Strip sat in the distance, gun and blaster fire intermittently illuminating the windows in the otherwise blackened hotel buildings. If this was not an isolated attack, like San Francisco had been, nothing was going to be operating normally for a very long time.

If ever again.

"It horrified K that the military had co-opted his machines," Terre said, shaking his head. He still struggled to comprehend how the kid was under this level of scrutiny. "There's no way he would have reactivated them to orchestrate another attack."

"That's why this rests on your shoulders, Hoffman. Find him. And if you can provide me with a better explanation, I'm all ears. Nobody knows these bots better than Mr. Klein. Figure out what he's attempting, but if he doesn't provide you with something extremely compelling, you're authorized to stop him at all costs."

Once again, the phone went silent without giving Terre a chance to argue.

At all costs? What was he now? A hitman?

Fredricks had to know Terre wouldn't shoot K if it came down to it.

Would he?

Terre slid the phone back into his pocket as he kept one eye on the Strip, which was still visible in his side-view mirror. The chaos had yet to settle down.

How does a country recover from a robot uprising? Terre

had no clue, especially when the US was so heavily reliant on tech. Most of the population would be useless without it.

And if he could get to K, would he do whatever it took to stop him?

Terre probed his memory, reflecting on the weeks he had spent with K in rehab; the weeks they had spent in Guam trying to fix proximity detectors; the day he'd spent with him on their wild ride through San Francisco, facing death and destruction at every turn in an attempt to stop the bots from destroying the city. Would K really have snapped to the point of undoing the peace they had experienced since?

Terre highly doubted it.

In that moment, Terre suddenly realized why Fredricks was pulling him in. The pieces clicked into place for the first time; the unspoken wink and nod in the conversation.

Fredrick's didn't believe K was capable of it, either.

And his old boss was right; nobody else knew K well enough to doubt his intent. If the US military wanted to take K out, they could have deployed a sniper or an assassin. Surely not *every* resource was occupied on the frontline. It wouldn't be hard to find someone if Terre couldn't get to the bottom of the situation.

Fredricks needed someone who wouldn't shoot first and ask questions later. And like it or not, Terre was that guy.

"Any news on your buddy?" Hailey asked. Another blockade of vehicles sat before them, and she turned a hard right, steering around the makeshift wall of cars up onto a sidewalk, around the obstacles, and back onto the road.

"Yeah," Terre said. "But no change in plans. We're still headed to the Hoover Dam to find out what he's up to."

Hailey focused her attention on the car's rearview mirror. Terre craned his head to catch a fireball exploding from the window of one of the hotel towers on the Strip. From where they were, he couldn't tell which building it was, only that a wayward flame must have hit something combustible, ignited, and took out a large swath of rooms along with it.

Hailey turned her attention back to him, her eyes squinted in disdain. "Sure would be nice to know what he's done to cause all this."

Chapter Two

Terre

The world was erupting all around them.

The Strip was engulfed in the echoes of explosions, gunshots, blaster fire, and shouts from police, military personnel, and those striving to evade them. In the strip malls, warehouses, and convenience stores that surrounded them, unrest was growing as frustrated citizens tried to make sense of the new world the bots had unwittingly plunged them into. But for Terre, all of it faded into the background of the night. In that moment, none of the calamity mattered.

It was the woman who sat next to him, driving him and the two women in the back seat into the night, that had his full attention. Hours ago, Hailey had just been a woman at a bar. She had sat next to him, seemingly by chance, ordered a pretentious cocktail, flaunted her newly manicured nails, and turned on the charm. Her complexion, only a shade lighter than his own, had reminded him of his late wife, Cara, which had left him vulnerable and willing to chat.

I should have gone back to my room.

That initial interaction had been a lie; a way to gain his trust. Hailey already knew of Fredricks's requests; that his ex-boss had assigned him to find his former colleague K. She was one of *them*—the Agency—and she was full of surprises. Like the CD-115 blaster she carried, or the road-illegal vehicle they now possessed.

And none of it sat well.

"Who are you?" Terre asked her abruptly. "Who are you really, and why are you here?"

Her face was impassive, her eyes focused on the road. "I'm here to ensure you don't get distracted. To ensure you fulfill your mission."

"*Bullshit*. Fredricks would have mentioned you."

"Who said Fredricks sent me? He doesn't have that kind of pull. But that doesn't mean people aren't listening to the noises he's been making. And in case you hadn't noticed, you're not exactly a trained operative, and for some reason you're the one being sent to stop a madman from kickstarting the apocalypse."

Terre gritted his teeth. "Kristopher Klein isn't mad."

"There's a besieged city behind us and a highway filled with empty vehicles that says otherwise."

"K might be a pain in the ass, but I've spent enough time alongside him to know he'd die before allowing himself to be the cause of this kind of destruction."

"It sounds like you're letting your relationship with Kristopher get in the way of your ability to think things through. Which is exactly *why* I'm here."

"And it sounds like you're letting the stick up your ass get in the way of yours."

Hailey pulled the steering wheel hard, nearly tipping the vehicle, to avoid a utility pole stretched across the road. Terre braced himself to avoid being flung out the window before Hailey jerked the car back onto the street, where the wall of immobile vehicles manifested before them forced them, once again, to slow to a crawl.

Hailey cursed under her breath as the SUV's headlights revealed row upon row of stationary cars stretching onward for as far as the light reached.

"We're going to have to find a side street," Hailey said, brushing Terre's comments aside.

"So, all hands are on deck, but they can spare you? What, they had no use for you other than as a babysitter?" Terre ignored the disarray of the road, intent on getting answers. "Fredricks just told me I'm being sent because there's no other option. Why bother sending me if I need further resources to watch my back? I didn't ask to be dragged into this."

Hailey flicked her gaze back and forth, searching for a way out of the mess, but it was near impossible to see any alternative in the dark. "There were no options that didn't involve taking your friend out." Hailey slowed the vehicle to a crawl. "*Something* I would have been all for, but, for whatever reason, Fredricks fought for your involvement. You shouldn't be the one being deployed—that much is clear—but here we are. If you can't—or *won't*—complete the mission, I'll make sure orders are executed."

Terre scoffed. Fredrick's words were still fresh in his mind. *You're authorized to stop him at all costs.*

"You're here to see that orders are executed? Or that *K* is?"

The flicker of hesitation in her eyes told Terre all he needed to know.

"I'll kill you, too, if I suspect you're in on this mess," Hailey responded coldly. "I have no qualms about doing what needs to be done. Whatever Klein's doing, it needs to end. The only thing saving your friend's ass is that he supposedly tried to help stop this attack to begin with."

"'Supposedly?'" Terre raised an eyebrow.

A break in the cloud cover allowed the moon to illuminate her features in the otherwise dark evening, enough for Terre to see her eyebrow lifting. "Does it look like the bots have stopped to you? You don't think there's a possibility he had this pre-planned?"

Terre paused, his mind racing for a reply. The words he found caught in his throat as he struggled to voice them.

She has no way of knowing, he reminded himself. *She wasn't there. She doesn't know—couldn't know—that the failure was mine, and mine alone.*

"You think this is because of him?" Terre managed. His stubble, both damp and coarse, chafed across his palm as he ran it over his face and into his hair. His shirt collar clung to his neck, and he loosened his top button to allow him to breathe easier.

"Can you give me a better explanation? Klein's the one who designed the original program, and he's the guy who was supposed to shut it down. It's barely been six weeks, and it's starting up again? It's pretty damn clear to me he sabotaged the upload."

Terre desperately wanted to defend his friend, but he couldn't offer Hailey a better explanation, not without admitting the truth. Not without disclosing that the upload had failed because of *him.* Terre had pulled the trigger on the Surge weapon that halted the upload prematurely.

The rearview mirror lit up as a fresh explosion rocked the Strip in the distance behind them.

Terre twisted in his seat to get a good look at the plume of smoke billowing from one of the hotels. The orbs above the city were still stationary, the jets still shadowing them in a holding pattern. Whatever was ravaging the Strip was ground-based.

Terre shook off the distraction. There was nothing they could do about the attack behind them.

Nothing except find K.

Maybe.

Terre imagined they'd find the guy and it'd be a big nothingburger. The programmer was probably catching his breath on the hiking trails of the Valley of Fire or around Lake Mead, away from people and away from tech. If so, K was a smart man. Terre wished he'd made the same decision rather than holing up in the Grand Kawa.

If Hailey wasn't hellbent on assassinating him, Terre would have been happy enough to leave his ex-coworker in her hands once they found him. Instead, he would need to take matters into his own hands. He'd never wanted to be involved anyway, but there had been no sidestepping Fredricks's orders. And if something was going on with Kristopher, Terre felt as though he at least owed it to the man to help him work it out.

But Terre found it staggering that Intel could have possibly dreamt up any scenario where the programmer had triggered this second wave of robot attacks. As if their own arrogance hadn't caused the whole thing.

He cleared his throat before he spoke. "K is a hero. If anything, he's the sole reason we've survived the past six weeks. If DARPA couldn't fix the ghosts in the machine, that's not on him."

"Well, you're lucky Fredricks felt the same way," she said. "But when your task fails, my job will be to clean up the mess."

Her dark eyes reflected the moonlight as Hailey gave him a sidelong glance. Terre wondered how she'd read the sweat on his brow and the quickening of his breath, but there was nothing he could offer her as an explanation. His guilty conscience had plagued him for weeks, but Terre still wasn't ready to come to terms with the failure of the upload. Not yet. Maybe never. And especially not to this woman, he wouldn't do himself any favors admitting to her that he was solely to blame.

Beyond the distant fighting, the streets were now mostly quiet. They had finally made it past the McCarran International Airport and the empty lots that surrounded it.

Terre had only been stationed at the Air Force base in Guam for a couple years, but it was still a shock to him that parking lots that once would have been filled to the brim now sat mostly empty. So few Americans owned vehicles anymore, relying instead on driverless rideshares picking up and dropping off their passengers to ease congestion. And with cars no longer sitting idle in garages and driveways, fewer needed to be produced, hence the empty lots.

In fact, Terre's own sedan back in San Francisco had been a rarity, and even he had no intention of replacing it after the bots had forced him to abandon it in the race to upload the Guardian Program.

Though the parking lots may have sat vacant, the vehicles that had to have been coming or going from the airport lined the freeway before them. There was just enough space for the SUV to slip between the two lanes of cars, and Hailey worked her way around until they reached an exit ramp, which she moved to take.

Terre wasn't familiar enough with the layout of Las Vegas to know where the exit led, but one thing he could tell by the curvature in the road was that it would be a detour from their current path.

"What are you doing?" Terre asked. "We need to keep going. It's the quickest way to the Dam."

"The freeway's not going to be the *quickest* way to get anywhere. Hundreds of people must have landed at the same time. I haven't seen the highways this jammed since automated traffic came into force."

Terre shook his head. He supposed Hailey was right. Whatever the AI had planned, jamming the highway was part of their strategy. Airports attracted congestion, and the bots had used that to their advantage. The tight lanes slowed them down, just as they were intended to stop military vehicles from rolling into the city.

"I'm assuming you know a faster route?" he asked.

"You keep talking shit as though you have some clue of how to do this better. If you know a better way past this, I'm all ears. If not, keep your mansplaining to yourself."

"We're being diverted intentionally. Keep going. Whatever's going on, I want to know why."

"It'll take us all night to get there at this rate! You know how little progress we've made since we left the Strip? This should have been a twenty-minute drive! We've been on the road for *two hours!*"

"Just stick with it a while longer. AI logic sets a route from which the units don't divert. If the protocols tell them to go that way because the route ahead is blocked, they take the exit. The beauty of human nature is, we're not always bound by the laws of logic. They *want* us to turn off. So, we ignore it and find what they don't want us to see."

Hailey muttered something under her breath that he didn't quite catch, though he was pretty sure it wasn't a compliment. They passed the exit, though, and Terre held his breath as he braced himself for whatever was coming next.

Chapter Three

Annika

I must be crazy.

Huddled in the back seat, Annika Phillips had tagged along with two strangers in an open-air SUV, with no way of knowing where she was headed or what their true intentions were. Only the promise that her sister Cheyenne wouldn't have remained in Las Vegas had swayed her to stay with them. The strangers were her ticket out of Las Vegas; her only chance to begin the search for her sister.

Annika had left Cheyenne in the care of their nanny bot, Ember. The Keeper's name was an obvious one, bestowed on the robot because of its bright red hair, intended to provide the unit with more humanlike qualities, and the orange glow to its eyes. At night, the robot's stare reminded Annika of a lit candle, faintly flickering in orange hues. An ember.

Ember had taken such a prominent place in their lives that, much to Annika's chagrin, Cheyenne thought of the bot as another big sister. Annika winced as she looked back on how she had allowed the machine to become central to her sister's well-being, but she'd had no other choice. It was that or have their family ripped apart.

Annika wouldn't have changed any action that meant they could remain together as a family.

Despite her certainty on that, Annika had agonized over allowing the bot to assume co-responsibility in raising Cheyenne. She was uncomfortable having the same base technology in their home to the systems that had ultimately led to her parents' death, but making use of the bot had meant it could take care of Cheyenne while Annika worked. Doing so meant giving Ember the freedom to drop her little sister off at school and pick her up after; it helped Cheyenne to study when Annika couldn't remember the first thing about grade seven math or the capital of South Carolina. So eventually she had to give way to reason

Annika did her best to be the best older sibling she knew how to be, but Ember brought order to their lives that Annika never could. The bot brought structure and discipline and a hundred and one ways to handle just about any situation raising a child might trigger.

Except now, the bot Annika had welcomed into their home, the bot she had entrusted with Cheyenne's safety and personal development, had kidnapped its charge and, according to Terre Hoffman, had likely marched her out into the middle of the Nevada desert.

Terre and his equally mysterious companion, Hailey Perkins, now sat in the front seat of their antiquated, gas-powered SUV, bickering just as they had ever since they'd left the Las Vegas Strip.

Annika had pretended to be asleep during the exchange. There was more happening out there in the desert than either of these two were letting on, and the churning in Annika's gut cautioned her against trusting either of them.

Her friend and coworker, Becky Johnson, snored beside her. Annika was relieved the woman was finally getting a reprieve. They had both endured a harrowing day, but Becky had been suffering from late-stage heatstroke, and without rest, the woman would soon be as good as dead. Annika didn't know what awaited them on the road ahead, but she did know Becky wouldn't be able to sit the next one out.

The empty vehicles stopped along the freeway, blocking them every few hundred yards, slowing them down; an eerie premonition that suggested the bots had a sinister plot unfolding. Terre had confirmed Annika's suspicions that the vehicles were not placed at random; they were supposed to slow down survivors. Sometimes, cars they came across were lined up, sitting side by side without even an inch between them. Annika wondered how far the effect of whatever had stopped the autonomous cars reached. Had all vehicles across the state stopped? Across the country? Across the world?

The stretch of road leading out of Vegas was mostly commercial. Small fires and emergency lighting cast eerie shadows against an enormous grocery warehouse beside them. Big box stores that had once needed parking lots now relied on pickup and drop-off lanes for driverless cars. Things were different in rural Saskatchewan, with small communities and farmhouses being spread too far apart for ridesharing to be realistic, so the concept was still alien to her. Now, though, empty cars lined the access road leading to the large-scale grocery store, waiting for passengers who weren't coming. The mass outage affecting the average person's mode of transportation that would make every prepper uncle she had say "I told you so."

If there was any relief to be had, it was in the first signs of people off the Strip. It seemed so strange for the streets to be barren, but the plumes of smoke rising from the Strip and giant robot orbs traversing the sky had drawn cautious onlookers from their homes and places of business. Where the evacuees from the Strip had vanished to, Annika could only guess, but the further they drove from the carnage, the more signs of life became apparent.

Any relief she felt, however, quickly disappeared once Annika realized the people she saw running in and out of the store were nothing more than looters.

Some of the more astute survivors were pushing carts loaded with food between the empty vehicles, presumably trying to stock their pantries until the robot apocalypse had ended. Others didn't seem to grasp the concept of what was going on, leaving the store with large-screen TVs, virtual reality systems, and other electronics that would be utterly useless and of no value if the power never returned.

Her mouth sat agape as Annika watched it unfold. Somehow, through every other disaster she had witnessed— the fires, the floods, even the attack on San Francisco—there had been a sense that the world would press on.

This felt different somehow.

Perhaps it was the trauma she had just gone through in escaping a terrorist attack in the middle of a robot insurgence, but something in the air told Annika that nothing would be the same again, and the people in the streets felt it, too.

Desperation marred their wide-eyed faces, some pulling children alongside them; kids whose arms were loaded up with toilet paper and other essentials. Annika imagined it wasn't a good idea to take your children to grab essential merchandise unless out of a desperate fear.

She couldn't help but picture herself and Cheyenne in the place of those scared families. How would they react? Would they, too, be forced to take whatever they needed to survive?

That thought hinged on Annika knowing where Cheyenne was. Right now, she had no idea whether her sister was even still alive.

At least those families had something to hold on to, even if it was just toilet paper.

"They're going to figure this out, right?" Annika's facade of sleep had disappeared with her gawking out the window. "The military must have something in mind to bring these bots under control?"

Annika didn't know all the details surrounding their current situation—why the power had failed or why the cell service had ceased—but she felt sure she was watching the potential collapse of what was once the most powerful nation on earth.

Could it truly be that bad? Or was this more isolated than Terre and Hailey had led her to believe? Annika had spent the whole day running, searching for her sister, only to turn up empty-handed. Over the course of that entire day, she hadn't really stopped to think about the implications of the destruction taking place around her.

Now, it all came rushing back, threatening to knock the wind out of her.

Her coworker Bruce had been killed by the bots on the Strip. The machine had fired a laser gun; something Annika had only seen in science fiction movies. Flashbacks of weapons fire whipping past her head, landing on others within the casino and on the street, and dozens of tourists fleeing for their lives as white-chromed soldier bots came storming through the city, filled her mind.

And then there had been the terrorists who had kidnapped her and left her to explode into a million pieces as their homemade detonation device ticked down in violent protest to the automatons stealing jobs and invading the city.

As Annika wrestled with the events of the day, it was hard to argue that Harold and Frank were wrong. Though their actions were deplorable, their premise, at least, was sound. Perhaps the world did need a wake-up call about their reliance on artificial intelligence and technology. It seemed, however, that their actions came too late.

The city of Las Vegas, once the Neon Capital of the

World, was in complete ruin because of humanity's reliance on artificial intelligence—and Annika didn't know if the rest of the world was faring any better.

Whatever their motive, whatever the hill they had decided to die on, the group of terrorists Frank and Harold had been part of had caused more harm than good. Whoever had orchestrated the attack was just another unnamed group with the power—or at least, the will—to wreak terror on the masses. They could have decided not to detonate those bombs; to prevent a secondary threat on a day already wrought with violence.

By choosing violence, they were just as heinous as the bots they sought to destroy.

Annika's question to her companions in the front seat hung in the open-air, the void of discussion looming as though she'd asked which among them had to die first. The roar of the gas engine, the shouts of looters, and the distant detonations all echoed into the otherwise still evening.

She couldn't help but glance over her shoulder. Smoke still swirled from the Strip, visible above the otherwise dark city only because of the flames that continued to burn below and the streaks of red and blue light from police vehicles.

A flash of light up ahead caught Annika's eye, and she strained her neck to get a better look. Her heart raced as the surrounding people appeared more and more agitated, desperate for the goods that were likely dwindling in supply. If people got too upset, she wondered how long it would be before they themselves became targets. Luckily, though they had garnered some attention, the onlookers hadn't threatened to approach them.

Apparently, the thought crossed Terre's mind as well. "We're in the thick of it now," he said, directing his words to Hailey. "We should get off the main roads altogether."

Moments ago, he had berated her for wanting to turn off

the freeway. The change in tune would have been humorous if the looters on either side of them hadn't been gazing in their direction.

"Oh, now you want to get off the main road!" Hailey said, her voice dripping with sass. "What happened to wanting to defy AI logic?

"Well, maybe I was wrong."

"Yeah, maybe you were wrong." Hailey clicked her tongue as she turned the vehicle onto a side street.

Outside, flames lit a fast-food restaurant next to a strip mall off the side of the freeway. Vehicles that had been parked to obstruct traffic flow were now aglow as well.

"What's happening here?" Annika asked, despite her first question going unanswered. "Why have these vehicles been smashed?"

It didn't appear to be looters that had done the damage. Not all of it, at least. Cars had been driven into each other, and driven into the sides of buildings, utility poles, and other obstacles they should have been programmed to avoid. It was as if the cars had become a more aggressive force once they had left the proximity of the Strip, many now burning in a ghastly display of destruction. The looters were adding to the damage, perhaps irate that their methods of transportation had since turned deadly. There were signs of blood beside the vehicles, too, but if there were any dead among the wreckage, something had either moved or hidden them from view.

Shattered glass littered the road, both from the wreckage and passengers who had escaped their vehicles' suddenly violent grasp.

Annika's mind went back to Darla and Marlene, the two women she had freed from baking to death in a gridlocked vehicle at the Las Vegas Convention Center. Who knew if the two women were safe? Even without the Sentinels and the anti-AI terror attack, they had been in rough shape. They had gone off in search of a pool party right before the robot soldiers had started marching down the Strip. Perhaps they never even made it to their destination.

"Whatever it is, it isn't good," Hailey replied, scanning the damaged cars as their SUV bounced over some of the smaller wreckage.

"You have no idea, do you?" Terre asked.

"If you're looking for answers, there's only one person who can give you them to you, and hopefully we'll find him at the Dam."

Terre shook his head, unconvinced, but he didn't voice his concerns.

Giant orbs, lit with blue light spinning across their surface, flew overhead, causing Annika to gasp. The Onyx had been content to hover in the distance all afternoon, but now it appeared as if they were ready to pull closer to the city center.

Fighter jets roared somewhere over the city, and a brief shaking of the ground followed gunfire below them. Annika could only imagine what was happening in the distance, outside of her line of sight.

The occasional flare of light briefly illuminated the otherwise darkened Strip, creating silhouettes of the famous buildings and attractions that lined the boulevard.

How many people were on that street alone? Half a million? More? If the curfew imposed by the National Guard proved at all effective, most of the civilians would stay in the hockey arena and football stadium. More would be holed up in undamaged portions of the resorts, likely clinging to any hope they could muster of convincing themselves that this nightmare would pass.

More than half a million people trapped, effectively under siege. And she had just left.

A burst of flames ignited behind the windows of a big box

store behind them, and suddenly she was back on the country road in Saskatoon seven years ago. Fire consumed the edges of the woods around her, consuming neighboring farmhouses, the blaze's destructive force ending both the livelihoods and lives of those who called the farmland home.

That night, more than a hundred lives were lost. And, like tonight, she'd ran then, too.

How many more people would die here? It already had to be in the thousands. There were dozens of dead bodies Annika had ignored as they fled the Grand Kawa Hotel alone. There'd likely be thousands more.

How many people had she left behind this time? And how many who were still here were looting and setting fire to their own neighborhoods? How many would survive what was coming?

Annika pushed down all the doubt, all the guilt, everything that wormed its way through her mind.

None of it mattered, except for one thing.

Finding Cheyenne.

Annika wouldn't repeat the one unforgivable act she had committed that day in Saskatchewan: she wouldn't abandon family. She'd dive headfirst into the blaze if she had to, if it meant there was a sliver of hope of bringing her sister home.

According to Hailey, Ember had probably led Cheyenne into the desert. Supposedly. *Hopefully.* Annika had to cling to that. She'd leave the rest of the city to burn; leave the rest to fend for themselves in a roll of the dice to get her sister back. To hang on to the last bit of family she had.

A strange sound echoed through the night, tearing her from her thoughts; a rumble that Annika couldn't quite place. The sound was something between a buzz of insects and the roar of machinery. The noise was intense enough to resonate over the shouts and yells of the rioters and the call of the sirens coming from the city.

As their SUV slowed to a halt to work its way around a

bus that had been pushed onto its side, the ground rumbled beneath them.

As Annika turned to see what was causing the commotion, she realized they wouldn't be going anywhere.

Chapter Four

Annika

There had to be hundreds of them; metallic soulless beings with glowing blue eyes marching down the freeway like a band of undead soldiers.

And they were moving fast.

"We've gotta move!" Annika cried, slapping Terre's shoulder in the seat in front of her.

The action was unnecessary as Terre's attention had already been roused, and he mirrored her gaze out of the side of the SUV. "Oh, *shit!* Hailey, step on it!"

Before Terre had finished the command, the SUV lurched forward, but there was only so fast they could go, forced to work their way in between the shells of empty cars that lined the street.

A group of six vehicles stretched across the road, blocking their path through an intersection. Annika didn't know where they were or what direction they needed to go in, but she knew they'd have to get through the blockade to escape the machines approaching from behind.

Headlights from the vehicle blockade suddenly erupted in bright streams and Annika reflexively gasped, putting a hand up to block the sudden intrusion of light.

"What's happening?" she asked.

"Hang on!" Hailey yelled. "And wake up your friend. We might need to make a run for it."

Terre had his blaster in hand, his face dark with worry and concentration. Annika grabbed Becky's arm and shook it roughly. How the woman had been able to sleep through the chaos so far was beyond her.

Becky blinked a few times, unaware of the sudden change in urgency, and rolled over, pulling an arm over her head.

"No, Becks," Annika urged. "You've got to wake up."

Becky looked over her shoulder, her eyes narrowed as though annoyed at the intrusion on her sleep, but then recognition took hold. The light in her eyes returned as she focused on Annika and pulled herself upright.

"What's going on?" she croaked, grabbing a water bottle that she had tucked beside her earlier and taking a sip.

The ground beneath them shook, causing Becky to splash the water she had just opened over her face. She spat out the rest when she noticed the glowing eyes and blue panel lighting stretched for miles down the road.

Annika grabbed the SUV's frame to steady herself as Hailey did a rapid three-point turn, evading the awakening vehicles by maneuvering onto a side street.

"What are they doing?"

Annika realized she had voiced her query aloud when Terre replied, "Damned if I know." He pointed to an even narrower space in the alley. "Hailey, pull in there. Kill the engine."

"No way!" she responded indignantly. "We need to keep moving!"

"We're not going anywhere until these bots pass, and we don't want the extra attention. Those vehicles have something else in mind."

"How do you know they're not here for us?" Annika squeaked.

"*A hundred* armed soldiers for *one* SUV? These bots are being deployed for a purpose, but we're not it."

Hailey cursed under her breath as they rolled past a small parking lot and behind a large brick building.

They were barely a block from the main road. From where they were situated, next to a large, non-descript gray brick building, Annika couldn't make out much more than a vacant lot that sat across from them. Beyond that, it appeared there were residential homes, but their features were lost in the darkness. Whether they were still inhabited or if their occupants had stepped out to loot a convenience store, there was no way to tell.

Before San Francisco, Annika wouldn't have believed people would be so quick to steal, to set things on fire out of fear, or to take advantage of an opportunity that presented itself. She knew riots were nothing new, especially when other activities occupied police and other security personnel, but in her small Saskatchewan town, the closest thing to riots she had ever witnessed were some teenagers breaking a few store windows and setting a few vehicles on fire after their hometown team won a national hockey tournament. And that had been the talk of the country for weeks.

Then San Francisco happened. As if the rogue bot attack hadn't been enough, the city's own citizens had turned on each other. Even weeks later, the city was still grappling to get the supplies they needed in the aftermath.

There was enough of a break between the adjacent buildings to make out the nearby street they had just left. Annika could make out reactivated cars now clearing a path for the bots marching down the road, positioning themselves on sidewalks and in parking lots. They were orienting themselves in an orderly way, evenly spaced.

Programmed.

Annika ducked as gunshots flared into the night. Becky jumped, grabbing onto Annika's arm, her eyes popping as she watched the parade of marching soldiers. The hauntingly metallic military procession sent chills down Annika's spine.

Terre had opened the vehicle's door, as though half expecting to bolt. The man had proven he knew his way around these bots, so if he was worried, Annika knew she had a reason to panic. She slowly undid her seatbelt, trying her best not to make a sound, and then opened her own door, less stealthily, and the crack and creak of the metal frame caused Terre to jump and focus his intense, dark stare on her.

"Sorry," she whispered.

Terre shook his head as if to tell her not to worry, then put a finger to his lips and turned his attention back to the street.

Annika was thankful Terre couldn't see her cheeks flush as her eyes darted from him to the street and back to her companions.

More gunfire erupted, crushing her worries. A bump in the night wasn't going to be noticed by the assailants.

"You won't take us alive!" an unseen man shouted into the night.

"Fools," Hailey muttered, just loud enough for Annika to hear.

Annika opened her mouth to ask what she meant when the gates of hell opened.

Swathes of blaster fire descended upon the parking lot of a burger chain, evaporating several rioters who had been heckling the machines.

Shadows and specks of people scrambled for cover under the moonlight. More than one stayed behind, fumbling for guns they had tucked out of sight. Many of the scrambling men and women appeared to be armed, but they were still unprepared for the assault being unleashed. A handful stood defiant, despite the fate of those who had been vaporized only moments before. Some, perhaps slightly more intelligent, futilely ducked behind vehicles or palm trees; anything they could find before returning fire.

Most just ran screaming.

"*Get down!*" Terre barked as he ducked into the vehicle's interior. It didn't offer much protection, and if the bots strayed from their path, the SUV's frame wouldn't provide sanctuary for long, but it was better than being four sitting targets out in the open.

Annika couldn't help but try to get a glimpse of faces before they met their fate. In the dark, it was hard to see anything but shadow and the outlines of people before waves of blaster fire lit their horrified faces. She could almost hear the *thud* as they collapsed to the ground; one last glimpse of their life before it ended.

Her knees ached from squatting on the SUV's floor, and she squirmed to position herself more comfortably. No matter how she leaned or moved, though, she couldn't quite seem to find relief. She finally decided on hanging one leg out of the door she had cracked open and pulled the other close to her torso.

The gunfire ceased, and the rumble of the mechanical Sentinels was carried off into the distance. The shouts of men and women were noticeably absent, and the vehicles that had repositioned themselves off the roadway became dormant once again.

A dog barked somewhere in the desert and yells of survivors who were still somehow alive on the Strip carried through the distance, but the breathing of Becky, Terre, and Hailey were the most invasive sounds Annika could hear.

Terre and Hailey whispered something between themselves, which Annika only caught snippets of.

"We don't have any other option," Terre said, his voice rising slightly.

"And what if they start ...?" Hailey replied, but she lowered her tone so that Annika couldn't catch the rest.

Becky was curled up on the floor of the SUV next to her. Her breathing was more ragged than it should have been. Moonlight revealed marks from the SUV's interior ran across her face from resting it against the vehicle's doorframe as she slept.

"You okay, Becks?" Annika asked.

"Ask me again when there aren't bots shooting at people."

Annika sighed but only nodded in reply, wondering if that would ever be the case again. She turned her attention to the two agents in the front seat. "We need to go. We've lost so much time already. If Ember brought Cheyenne into the desert like you say, we need to get to them."

Hailey sighed, drumming her fingers on the steering wheel as though considering their next course of action.

"We need to stop for the night," Terre said. "We're not getting anywhere like this."

Annika bit her lip as she tried to process what Terre was saying. She had been shot at, kidnapped, narrowly escaped a hotel bombing, and had narrowly escaped a city being forced into lockdown. Their robot assistant had kidnapped her sister, and an army of death machines were marching the streets and circling above them—and now this man, this … *stranger* was telling her they were just going to sleep while Cheyenne was still missing?

"You can't be serious?" she protested.

"We're going to need to sleep at some point," Terre insisted. "It's getting dark, and we need to be able to see the obstacles laid out on the road ahead or we're not going to get anywhere. It will serve us better to rest, compose ourselves, and leave at first light." He looked at his watch, though Annika was sure he knew exactly what time it was. "It's nearly 9 p.m. That means first light is just over eight hours away. We need to be able to see and think clearly. There's too much going on we don't know about."

Annika struggled to keep visions of her sister out of her

head. Who knew what Ember had been up to while they were trying to find Cheyenne in the Kawa Resort, never mind now that they were out in the desert somewhere? And that was assuming Hailey had been right. What if the woman had misjudged the situation? What if Cheyenne and Ember had gone to the arena after all?

She put her palms to her face, rubbing her cheeks as her mind raced.

Annika looked incredulously at Hailey. Shadows played tricks on the woman's face from her extended eyelashes, and her face was softer than Annika would have expected, given the woman's no-nonsense attitude, but it betrayed no emotion; no hint as to what thoughts were being processed beneath the surface.

"Terre's right," Hailey said finally. That had been the last thing Annika had expected the woman to say under the circumstances, but she let the woman continue, too taken aback to interrupt. Hailey then turned to Terre. "Though I really wish it made sense to keep moving. We don't know what the next phase in Klein's plan is. The sooner we can take him out, the better. The bots won't wait around for daylight, and neither should we. Command wanted us to move in as quickly as possible, and I agree. We don't know what else he's planning."

"I've told you before," Terre replied, "Intel are wrong. K's not behind this. If he's up to anything, it'll be putting a stop to this, and trust me, I'll do nothing but get in his way."

"We have our orders!" Hailey's voice carried an air of command without raising in volume.

Annika fought back tears of frustration. She had come so far and wasn't going to give up now. There wasn't time to rest; to wait and see what the bots might do. She wouldn't sleep restfully until her sister was safe and sound.

"Your stupid programmer has nothing to do with me," Annika said, furrowing her brow. "I don't care about Vegas. I don't care about whatever issue the two of you have with your agency. I came with you because you offered to help find Cheyenne, not for a camping trip in a Walmart parking lot. If you want to stay here and wait until morning, knock yourselves out. But I'm not sticking around."

Chapter Five

Terre

Fredricks be damned.

Hailey be damned, for that matter. Whatever K was doing, it wasn't going to help anyone if they got themselves killed along the way.

Annika could make her own decisions. Terre still hadn't figured out what it was about the Canadian's plight that had led him to get involved in the first place, other than that their paths had seemed to lead them in the same direction, and he was happy to help the woman try to find her sister. But he already had more on his plate than he could ever have bargained for. Finding K was more of a diversion than he could handle at the moment.

The look in Annika's eye was telling, though. She'd do anything to save Cheyenne, and after everything that had transpired over the past few months, Terre couldn't blame her. But he also knew that being rash was going to get them into more trouble than it would help. There were more unknowns in the desert night than just the bots alone. He had seen the look on the faces of the people looting the stores along the side of the road. People were desperate, and when that happened, they became unpredictable.

And then, of course, there was the battalion of Sentinels that had just marched past them, or the other tech weapons out there that were equally deadly. Sentinels and Onyx looked intimidating, but the military owned an entire host of artificially intelligent drones capable of considerable lethality. If the bots had compromised all networks, Terre and his companions couldn't afford to take unnecessary risks. They had to take things one step at a time.

"Did you not just see the bots that marched by?" he asked. "You've seen what the Sentinels can do. And it will be worse at night. The darkness doesn't affect them. Benefits of thermal imagery. If you're in their way, they'll kill you before you even see them.

"Whatever's happening, it seems they're intent on marching *into* the city center. If we can lay low for the evening, hopefully they'll just pass us by. In the morning, we'll at least be able to see the cars we're trying to steer around, and that'll give us a fighting chance of not getting blown to bits in the process."

"And what if you're wrong? What if they're just starting at the center and working their way out? Are you willing to take that risk?" Annika persisted. "No, I'm not waiting. If you think we'll be in danger out there, what does that mean for Cheyenne? We need to find her." She reached for the handle of the SUV's door. "*I* need to find her.

Terre reached around his seat and grabbed her wrist, stopping her from pulling the latch. "If that bot of yours wanted your sister dead," he said, doing his best to keep his voice steady and its volume under control, "we would have found her body in your hotel room. It's keeping her alive. Which is what it was designed for. Contrary to everything else that's going on, we have to trust its programming. I'll bet Cheyenne's safer with Ember than she'd be with us. At least for now."

Terre hated guessing. He hated the idea of giving Annika false hope. Truthfully, he didn't know why the bot had taken the girl, but something K had said back in San Francisco had resonated with him. The robotics expert believed the Guardian Program would reset the military bots back to their default programming. If what was happening now had somehow affected the Keeper bot, then maybe it was still acting in the interests of protecting Cheyenne.

Maybe.

It was only a guess, but Terre thought it was a pretty damn good one. If the bot had turned homicidal, he'd bet his hefty Zatica Industry salary that the scene at the Kawa hotel room would have been very different.

Annika tried to twist away, but Terre held firm. "We have to go with the assumption the bot's still trying to protect her. That's the only way we're going to find her alive."

"So? Then what?" Annika snapped. "We're just going to sleep? What good is that going to do? Let some looters find us and kill us in our sleep? At least, even if we're moving slowly, we're still moving."

"It'll save gas for one," Hailey replied, changing her tune.

Terre didn't want to complain, but he had to admit he was caught off guard by her backing him up on this one. He tried to study her with what little light was coming into the cab. Hailey hadn't turned her gaze from the windshield until that point, but she twisted in her seat now to look at Annika.

"If we're crawling along all night, having to backtrack and work around unseen detours," Hailey continued, "we're going to burn through a lot of unnecessary gas. I hate to admit it—I'd like to press on as well—but I'd rather this wasn't a one-way trip."

Terre caught the woman's eye as she gave him a sidelong glare. Her hands gripped the steering wheel, tighter than they needed to in the stationary vehicle, and her jaw was clenched. Hailey might not like the idea, but he'd take it. If Sentinels were marching down the freeways, he'd rather have the advantage, however slight, of daylight. Maybe Hailey was coming to that conclusion as well.

Annika snorted. "I'm not leaving her."

She twisted out of Terre's grip, pushed the door open, and stepped out, stumbling slightly as her boots hit the ground. She regained her balance by placing one hand on the car frame.

"You're going to go alone?" Terre asked.

Annika stopped and met his gaze. Her features were barely visible in the moonlight, but Terre swore he could see the heat of the woman's anger.

"I've been going it alone my entire life," she said. "I don't need you. I don't need *anyone* looking out for me. Get over yourself and your savior complex. I'll be fine."

Annika slammed the door of the vehicle and took off down the road into the night.

Terre swore under his breath.

"Let her go," Hailey said, just as Terre had grabbed the latch to open his own door. He paused in response. Adrenaline raced through his veins as his breathing quickened.

Why is this bothering me so much?

He heard the other rear door open and close behind him, much more gracefully than Annika's had. Despite Becky remaining silent during the heated exchange, it didn't surprise Terre that Annika's best friend would join her. There was no sense in trying to talk her out of it.

"Are we going or staying?" Terre asked Hailey. "I'm actually surprised you're siding with me on this one."

"We *should* keep moving," she said. "And I wish we could. But, as much as I hate to admit it, you're right. As long as those robots keep marching past us instead of hunting us down, it makes the most sense to wait out the night. We can take turns keeping watch."

"And what about Annika and Becky?" Terre asked. "We're just going to let them go?"

"It's not our call, Terre" she said evenly. "And besides,

she's right; nobody made you her hero. You bumped into a young woman on the street who reminded you that bots killed your daughter and made it your God-granted mission to stick your big dumb butt into her business."

How much did this woman know about him? He supposed his wife's death in the attack on Guam would have been part of her debriefing, but it was still unnerving to hear his wife's death used against him. Terre opened his mouth to argue, but Hailey kept going.

"Don't even begin to argue, Terre. I was there with you. I almost got killed because you decided you were Spider-Man or something. We gave them the option to join us, and frankly, that's more than we should've done. Let her go. She's not yours to save."

Terre nearly choked on the words. The woman didn't know the first thing about him or his intentions. So what if he wanted to help? So what if he knew what it was like to lose family to the bots? Was he supposed to stand back and do nothing? Just watch while innocent people died? He knew Annika had looked after herself and Cheyenne until this point, but the bots hadn't been a threat to them then. Nobody had dealt with them on the same level as he had.

Almost nobody.

"I know you want to help," Hailey continued, resting a hand on his. Her skin was smooth, and her touch sent a spark through his arm as though it were electrically charged. If Hailey noticed the bolt of energy, she didn't let on or shift her grip. "But the only way *you* can help is to get Klein to stop."

Would Terre be able to make that happen if it came down to it? He might have shared a couple of traumatic experiences with the kid, but he'd hardly considered K a close friend. He wasn't even sure Kristopher would hear him out once they found him. Terre hadn't seen the programmer since they'd left San Francisco. And seeing as though uploading the Guardian Program hadn't gone so well, Terre had no reason to assume this time would be any different.

He knew Hailey was trying to keep him on task, focused on the bigger picture, but leaving Annika to her fate still didn't sit right with him.

"You're telling me you don't care what happens to her out there?" he pressed. "Bots, looters, terrorists ... She has no way to protect herself."

"You think I'm heartless?" Hailey asked, removing her hand from his. The coolness of the night against his skin made the space feel emptier than he'd cared to admit. "You think she's the only one in this mess? Look around you, dumbass. You see those people stocking up on goods in the warehouse? Sure, some of them are opportunist thieves, but most of them are just trying to give their loved ones a fighting chance. You think they didn't see what happened in San Francisco? There are still food shortages six weeks later! What about *those* people's kids? What about protecting *them*? Why are you so hellbent on protecting *this* woman? You like her or something? Otherwise, it makes no sense to me why you'd go running off into the night after her."

Terre huffed. If he were honest with himself, he didn't have an answer as to why he felt responsible for Annika.

Hailey was right. Annika was perfectly capable of making her own decisions and was in no worse of a predicament than the thousands of other Sin City survivors now doing all they could to prepare for an impending doomsday.

"It's not like *that*," Terre said. "I guess something about her struck a chord. Like a calling I couldn't ignore. I just wish I could've convinced her to wait it out, you know? We'll all be fresh in the morning. I'm just trying to do what's best."

"If it was your daughter," Hailey said, "would you listen when some dude you just met told you to wait out the night? Would you sit around wondering what had become of her? Or would you continue? On your own, danger be damned?"

Terre sighed. He knew the answer. If he could go back in time, he would have done anything to rescue Sarah. Even as the drone strike continued to hammer down on the base in Guam, his own safety would never have entered the equation. He would have run back into their home while the missiles were falling all around him, for the one chance to save her.

Hailey was also right in that he didn't have any reason to feel any more responsible for Annika than anyone else who was suffering the same fate. How many loved ones were currently separated from each other with no contact? With no way of knowing if their families were okay, safe within an evacuation center, or blown away by a Sentinel blaster?

Terre shook his head. He knew staying put for the night was the logical answer and that he should let Annika go. She was little more than a stranger to him. But he also knew he couldn't. He hadn't kept her alive this far to have her die in the middle of the desert. Walking to the Hoover Dam would be a stretch on the best of nights.

"I know you're right," he said. "But I'm still going after her."

He pushed open the car door, despite the exasperated sigh from Hailey.

"Terre, wait!"

Terre paused as his leather shoes hit the ground. Not because Hailey had asked him to, but because he didn't know in which direction Annika had gone. He scanned the visible area, but the night enveloped pretty much everything.

"Annika!" he shouted.

"*Terre!*" Hailey hissed. "*Quiet!*"

Chapter Six

Cheyenne

Cheyenne Phillips had been walking for hours. Ember—once her guardian, now her captor—prodded her from behind.

The moon and stars provided some illumination on the desert landscape, yet all Cheyenne could see was the rocky terrain in front of her. She still had no indication of where they were going, or how long it would take to get there.

They had kept to the road. Cars moved out of their way, offering a path, as if the two lone figures were the Israelites crossing the Red Sea. And though Cheyenne wasn't sure, she had a feeling the self-driven vehicles closed the path behind them again after the convoy had passed.

A convoy of bots and machines.

Hundreds of automated devices walked, rolled, and maneuvered down the road. The highway was nearly void of natural life. The only sign that there might once have been people among the discarded metal shells was the occasional door flung open, jutting onto the freeway.

Crickets chirped, accompanying the metallic grind of gears and circuits traveling over the interstate.

There were other people being led into the desert besides Cheyenne, but the bots had kept them so far apart, she had only caught glimpses of them before the sun went down. Everyone she had seen appeared to be a teenager or younger, though at a distance, it was hard to tell.

The events after the power outage had mostly been a blur for Cheyenne. But she clearly remembered Ember throwing her down on the bed in a fit of defiance the robot had never shown before.

Cheyenne hadn't thought the robot had tossed her that hard, but she must have blacked out for at least a few minutes. When she came to, her head was pounding. It took a few moments for the room in the Grand Kawa Hotel to come into focus.

As the blur of movement around her dwindled, Cheyenne's memories returned.

The power outage. The crowd blocking the entrance to the hotel. Trying to leave the suite to find food and her sister. Then she was falling. A pile of blankets and mattress beneath her softened the blow, but somehow darkness still overtook her.

As she came to, Cheyenne paused briefly. Rolling herself over, the softness of the blankets discounted that her robot Keeper had just turned on her. Seconds ticked by as she tested her arms. Each appendage seemed to do its job, but Cheyenne couldn't bring herself to face the robot in the room, unsure of what reality would be waiting for her.

Ember had never tried to attack her before. Had the robot misjudged its own strength? Had a malfunction or glitch sent her flying, rather than simply blocking her path? Or was something else going on?

For seven years, Ember had done nothing but protect and encourage Cheyenne. For the machine to behave in any other way didn't make sense to Cheyenne.

There was a dull ache in her shoulder from where the bot had grabbed her, but she resisted the urge to rub the bruise. She had to determine what was happening before making any sudden moves.

Cheyenne risked turning her eyepiece on. Perhaps if the service had been restored, she could get a message to Annika. Or the police.

Anyone, really.

But zero bars greeted her as the projected screen came to life. Frustrated, Cheyenne brought her finger up to turn off the device once again. She might as well preserve battery, just in case she was able to use the device later.

Cheyenne turned over and decided she needed to get a better look at the room. Her backpack was resting next to her. It hadn't been on the bed previously. Ember must have moved it. She sat up, surveying the space that now seemed to be her prison.

Ember had ornately cleaned everything and packed hers and Annika's bags. The robot had made the bed and returned everything to its rightful place, as though nobody had been staying in the room at all.

But Ember was nowhere to be seen.

It wasn't like the bot to have left her alone, but Cheyenne wondered for a moment if the bot had abandoned her. Given the circumstances, perhaps *that* wouldn't be the worst thing that could happen to her.

A popping sound echoed from the street outside her window. Cheyenne thought it might have been gunfire. She'd heard enough from her father's hunting rifle back when they'd lived on the farm to recognize the sound. Why anyone would be firing outside was beyond her, but Cheyenne made her way over to the windows that stretched from floor to ceiling at the edge of her room.

The sun had yet to set, which told her she hadn't been unconscious for long; an hour, at most. The wall of protesters hadn't lessened; in fact, it appeared to have grown exponentially. Cheyenne recalled the hotel had locked its doors—or at least, that's what Ember had told her—so the swell was likely the result of hundreds of people unable to get back to their rooms. She was certain Annika was among them, probably freaking out about her little sister being in the room on her own.

If it wasn't for Ember's erratic behavior, Cheyenne might have criticized Annika for being so worried about her, as she often was. But in that moment, it was a fear that might well be warranted, depending on where the bot had gone to.

Signs and billboards that would normally be illuminated stood dark, and Cheyenne realized the power was still out all the way down the Strip. Movement caught her eye as the crowds parted and then scrambled to get free of whatever was approaching down the road.

A group of stark white beings marched down the middle of the boulevard. Cheyenne gasped as blue light erupted from the weapons they held, striking people in the crowd.

A black tank followed behind the six bots, so dark that it was almost impossible to see against the black asphalt beneath it. It plowed through cars, clearing its own path.

The display was so foreign that Cheyenne struggled to understand what she was looking at. She had seen a few bots that looked like Ember before, but this group came worryingly close.

The approaching robots had humanlike faces and white-paneled bodies, but that was where the similarities with Ember ended. These bots were buff, as if built for intimidation, and had no hair. Ember's most distinguishing feature was the bright red hair that decorated its head, flowing down its back in a flamboyant attempt for it to appear more lifelike.

Perhaps this was a parade, she thought; some sort of event that Annika forgot to mention to her.

But Cheyenne knew that as fantastic as that would be, it wasn't true.

These bots were the same design as the ones that had attacked San Francisco last month; the ones Cheyenne had seen on the news. Except these were on the street below her hotel room, and the ones on the news had also been capable of flight. She quickly scanned the skies but saw nothing.

Smoke drifted from the black tank for a moment before it erupted in a spark and puff of smoke. The discharge shook the building, but the impact of the projectile it unleashed shook it more, and Cheyenne's mouth dropped in horror as the pedestrian bridge forty-eight floors beneath her window exploded, sending bodies and chunks of debris soaring into the street. The force sent swaths of people flying into stalled vehicles, neighboring buildings, or vegetation.

"It's time to go," a familiar mechanical voice chimed from behind her.

Cheyenne had heard Ember's speech synthesizer thousands of times before, but it now sounded different somehow; hollow, offering command rather than suggestion. The robot's tinny voice had always seemed empathic and caring, on the surface at least. Suddenly, her Keeper's tone was no more concerned than the voice assistant on her eyepiece. The statement was utilitarian, as though unconcerned with Cheyenne's state of well-being.

It also wasn't a suggestion.

Choices quickly and quietly skirted the edge of Cheyenne's consciousness. She was still woozy and trying to get her bearings. She nearly lifted a hand to her shoulder, where the bruises from her latest act of defiance still bore the Keeper's mark.

If she refused, Cheyenne had no doubt Ember would knock her out and swing her over its shoulder. If she complied, perhaps she'd be able to escape along the way.

Maybe. In order for an opportunity to present itself, Cheyenne needed to be alert.

She didn't have a choice.

"Where are we going?"

"To safety," the bot replied. "Collect your bag. It has already been packed for you."

They were just about out of the city's limits when the earth shook.

Cheyenne risked a look back, and even with night falling, she could make out the smoke rising from the direction of the Strip. There was no way for her to know for sure what had caused the explosions, but after seeing both the tanks and Sentinels in action, she had a pretty good idea.

None of it mattered, though. Las Vegas had only existed for her for a few days. Before this week, it hadn't been a place she could see, hear, and smell. It had been nothing more than a song; a setting on TV; an idea filled with Elvis impersonators, slot machines, and, lately, robot workers.

Robot workers, who now seemed to have rebelled or malfunctioned, or maybe they'd just had enough of serving drinks, dealing cards, and re-painting walls; all the things the robots did without their human owners thinking twice.

Except Cheyenne really had no idea if that was the case. Just like she didn't know why the exodus of bots was taking place. She had no idea why the white robots were attacking people in the street or why fighter jets flew overhead. Everything had escalated beyond Cheyenne's comprehension.

As the city burned around her, Cheyenne knew that, against all odds, the safest place for her to be was *with* the robots. In her mind, as long as she was with Ember, at least the white bots weren't shooting at *her*.

Wherever Ember was leading her, Cheyenne didn't know, but so far, it was *away* from all the destruction. That had to count for something, right?

If she stood any chance of escaping, she had to be away from all the dangers of the city before attempting it.

Beside them, other bots rolled down the freeway as driverless cars started and moved out of their way. Somewhere ahead of them, larger pieces of machinery, all automated, rumbled down the road. Construction equipment and workhorse machines led the way out of the Promised Land and into the desert, like Moses, but in reverse.

"Where are we going?" Cheyenne asked for what felt like the hundredth time since they'd started out. Her throat was raw from the desert air and lack of water. They'd been walking for hours, and Cheyenne had no clue as to how long the trek might last.

"You're in need of water," Ember said. It was the most the bot had spoken since they had left the hotel. A canteen appeared in the bot's hands, seemingly out of nowhere. "Drink."

It sounded like more than a suggestion, but at that point, Cheyenne didn't care. She grabbed the bottle and poured the contents down her throat, feeling the cool water soothing the dryness within.

"We are going somewhere safe," Ember answered. "We will protect you."

Cheyenne would have paused at the answer if the bot would have let her. Suddenly, the old tone of her bot had returned; calm and empathetic, as if it really cared about her well-being.

What was with Ember? Cheyenne still had many unanswered questions. She was unsure of where she was going; unsure if Annika was alive; unsure if the last thing she'd see was a sea of robots marching her to her death through the desert.

She didn't know why Ember wasn't giving her a straight answer—Cheyenne would have thought intentionally being vague would have gone against her programming—but perhaps finding their destination, a place of safety, was occupying all of the bot's processing power. Perhaps the dust of the desert was interfering with its circuits.

Cheyenne rolled her eyes as she handed the canteen back to the bot. She was tired of asking, and she didn't seem to be in danger here. She just wished she could tell Annika where she was. Most of all, she wished she knew if Annika was alive.

But Cheyenne did know one thing for certain: if her sister was still alive, Annika wouldn't rest until she found her.

Chapter Seven

Annika

Annika stumbled more than once as she crossed the rugged terrain. Her heart slammed against her chest after only a few minutes of pushing her new hiking shoes against the asphalt. Becky was right on her heels, doing surprisingly well, considering how the rest of her day had gone. Her face was flush, but she wasn't breaking a sweat, seemingly comfortable at the breakneck pace Annika was setting.

But as Annika ran, her anger tempered, and she realized that as much as she wanted to find Cheyenne as quickly as possible, she didn't want to injure her friend in the process. It would be so easy to push as hard as she could, for as long as she could, but she didn't truly know how far *she* could sustain the pace, let alone her friend, who had spent most of the evening wiped out and curled up on the upholstery of the SUV. But she knew Becky would push herself past her limits to keep up, which wouldn't do either of them any good.

Annika eased her pace, slowing to a walk to allow Becky the chance to catch her breath. Any coolness her movement had brought with the wind against her skin instantly stagnated, and the warm air clung to her, cloying against the blouse and dress pants she now so desperately wished she could change out of.

At least she had changed her shoes in the hotel room. Becky's feet were still adorned in the flats she had worn to the conference, causing Annika to cringe with guilt. Dust caked their surface, and they would provide little comfort against the harsh terrain of the desert. Annika could only imagine the shin splints the woman would endure if forced to run on them for more than a kilometer.

And they had so far to go. The immensity of the journey ahead suddenly weighed on her. Without the normal light pollution of the city, the sky seemed endless. The stars were like blinking lights of eternity—impossibly far away, hidden by the city's neon lights for a century—now, for the first time in human memory, visible in the Las Vegas night sky.

"You don't need to follow me," Annika said as Becky approached. "Not that I don't appreciate it, but I know you probably need the rest. I won't hold it against you if you decide to stay with the others."

Becky smiled as she caught her breath. The woman was panting, but not to the point of gasping. The little rest she had received on the road had given her a bit of her stamina back.

"Has there ever been a time when you haven't had my back? Cheyenne's almost as much my sister as she is yours."

Annika nodded. Becky had always been there when she and Cheyenne had needed a hand. Likewise, Annika had helped her friend out of more than one jam. But it was nothing like this. Nothing like jogging through the desert in the middle of the night with killer robots, looters, and crazed CIA agents lurking around every turn.

"This is different, though, Becks. I wouldn't be able to live with myself if something happened to you, too."

"*Hey!*" Becky put her hands on her hips. "I'm capable of

making my own choices. You don't have to feel responsible for my safety. I'm here to help, not to be babysat."

Annika sighed. Becky was one of the most capable people she knew. It was easy to forget, working behind a desk all day, that both of them had grown up on a farm and had learned how to deal with the unexpected from a young age.

"No, you're right. Sorry. I'm just a little on edge after the day we've had."

"I get it. But remember, we started out this day together, and we're going to finish it together."

Becky squatted on the sidewalk, putting a hand down to give her feet a reprieve. She bounced as though she still had energy, but Annika wondered how far the woman was realistically going to be able to push herself. "Are we really going to try and run the entire way there tonight?"

Annika crossed her arms and, for the first time since they stopped their run, studied the empty parking lot next to where they stood. They were still far enough from the main roads that the looters were nowhere to be seen. Dogs barked in the distance, along with the yells of looters and the injured. The cars in the lot seemed to be parked in designated stalls, stationary until called upon. Whether they were there by command or if these were their normal parking spaces, it was impossible to say. They were dormant for the time being, and that was all Annika cared about.

A small group of people, possibly homeless, huddled around a makeshift fire a half-block away. A few vehicles sat close to them, though, so it was possible they had just decided to make the most of their situation and camp at the back of an old mechanic shop.

The road itself stretched beside them and into darkness. Annika assumed it would eventually wind back onto a primary route and, from there, onto the freeway, but she really had no idea.

A million miles seemed to lie ahead of them, and Annika

didn't know what to think anymore. She had never been to the Hoover Dam—assuming that was where Cheyenne was being held—but she had looked at day tours to the site. They had been entirely booked for the week, so she and Cheyenne never got the chance to go, but Annika remembered from their website that the dam was an hour away by bus. She didn't know what that equated to on foot, but she imagined it would take the better part of the night.

Suddenly, waiting until morning didn't seem like such a ridiculous idea.

"*Shit*," she thought aloud as she rested her hands on her thighs. She doubled over as her mind reeled. "Maybe this was a stupid idea after all."

"What is?" Becky asked. "Sorry, I didn't mean to … Are you okay?"

Annika nearly fell over as she let out a full burst of laughter. It felt like a ridiculous reaction, but it spilled out of her in uncontrollable waves until she was howling into the night.

Becky approached and rested a hand on her shoulder. "You're scaring me."

"I'm …" Annika managed between spurts. "… I'm okay …"

Even in the evening's darkness, it was apparent that Becky had raised a skeptical eyebrow.

"No …" Annika said, bringing the laughter under control, wheezing as she struggled to control her breathing. "No, I'm really *not* okay. There's *nothing* about this that's okay. I'm overtired. The ridiculousness of the question just struck me." Annika struggled with the explanation, even to herself. "This has to be the shittiest day since my parents died. It might even be worse."

Annika took a deep breath, letting the enormity of the day crash all around her.

Becky stood motionless, her big blue eyes reflecting the moonlight. Her chest shook with each breath, though whether that was from the recent sprint or from the concern for her friend, Annika couldn't say.

"I think I made a mistake," Annika said, the fit of laughter all but gone. How could she have acted so rashly? She took another deep breath, allowing the dry desert air to scratch her throat and lungs before she exhaled the immensity of the quest that lay before her.

"Becky, I don't know what the answer is. I need to find Cheyenne, but this was a dumb move. How could I be so stupid? What? We're going to walk to the Hoover Dam? Walk through the night and be too tired to be of any use by the time we get there? We'll be further behind than we would be if we'd stay the night."

Becky nodded and stared into the desert, as though pondering their fate. "Well," her friend said, "we know Terre and Hailey were going to stay put. Let's just head back. No harm done. Our egos might be bruised, but we'll still get a night's rest. It might give us some perspective."

Running in a blind rage, Annika hadn't thought to keep track of their steps and hadn't paid close enough attention to retrace them. She didn't have to voice her complaint; Becky simply nodded, as if she knew her friend well enough to understand the error, and stepped off in the direction from which they came.

Why am I so stupid? Annika kicked a nearby rock, sending it into the side of a concrete partition in the adjacent parking lot. The noise caught the attention of a small group of degenerates that had been huddled around a fire lit in a garbage barrel; two men and a woman, aglow in the flame's reflection, previously unconcerned with the two young women.

Annika caught her breath as the glowing faces turned their way. Recognition struck her in the gut as though someone had sucker-punched and knocked the wind clear out of her. Suddenly, she realized she had made a colossal error in judgment.

She should have stayed with Terre. She shouldn't have run. She definitely shouldn't have kicked that rock. But it was too late now.

"Why, hello, gorgeous." A Southern accent called into the night as the man closest to them stood from his makeshift seat of wooden pallets. His voice was akin to nails on a chalkboard. Taunting, teasing, and telling her, *I told you so.*

"It's nice to see you've found us."

In the fire's glow, Harold, the man who had kidnapped her in the stairwell of the Kawa hotel, flashed a dark and toothy grin.

"*Run!*" Annika hissed at Becky as she turned, her feet churning gravel as she tried to gain traction. Dirt flew behind her until her boots found their footing.

Annika caught a glimpse of Becky's wide-eyed, slack-jawed expression. The crease on the woman's forehead indicated she clearly had questions about the turn of events, but she started moving regardless, realizing the gravity of Annika's orders.

They didn't make it more than a hundred meters before Becky yelped against the sound of an electronic *buzz* and *pop*. Seconds later, another *pop* resounded, and Annika felt a sharp sting against her left calf. The rest of her collapsed beneath her as her muscles lost all strength. Pain flashed in her vision as Annika hit the ground, unable to lift her hands to stop the rocky ground from slamming into her face. A thousand cuts stung her as the gravel scraped against her knees, belly, chest, and face.

Pain rushed through her skin, filling her senses. Annika could only imagine that rock fragments had embedded themselves into her flesh. Her arms refused to respond to her commands. She had to push herself up; had to move.

But it was to no avail.

Harold must have shot me. Could he have paralyzed me? She hadn't felt a bullet. But in spite of that, she had never been shot before—perhaps the electrocuted sensation was what being shot through a nerve felt like.

A chill ran through her and her muscles twitched involuntarily, sending Annika into spasms that lurched her further along the pavement.

I'm going to die, she thought. *This is how it ends.*

A heavy boot landed on her hip, roughly kicking her over onto her back.

Harold stood above her, a weapon in one hand still sparking blue. The pieces of what had happened started to form. The man had shot her, but not with bullets—he had used a Taser of some sort.

Becky let out a cry behind her, but Annika couldn't lift her head to check on her friend. She opened her mouth to call out, but she could only manage a croak.

"Well, how'd you get here? I thought you were toast." Harold smiled. "I guess it doesn't matter. I knew we'd get to have our fun," There was a wobble in his stance that told her the man hadn't sobered up since their last encounter. "And you brought a friend. How thoughtful."

Harold moved so that he was out of her direct line of sight—not that Annika wanted to see the bastard again. The less she had to see of the lowlife scum, the better off she was. But all Annika could see was stars above her, and it was terrifying not to be able to see the threat that stood right at her side.

All her focus diverted into trying to make her limbs move. After a few moments, Annika could wiggle her fingers and then the toes on her right foot, but it was a concerted effort. Making a break for it wouldn't be in the cards any time soon.

The rise and fall of her chest gave her some comfort over her physical state, but not much. The effects of whatever Harold had hit her with at least appeared as though they might be temporary.

"And who's this fine young angel you brought with you? She's just about as pretty as you are."

"*Let her go!*" Annika yelled, as well as she could manage, into the void of the night. Her voice trembled as she spoke. "I'll do whatever you want, but just let her go!" She cringed as she said the words.

Feeling was slowly returning to her limbs, enough so that she could slowly move her legs. They were heavy, but muscle movement was returning. Tears flowed freely onto the dirt beside her. Annika tried to hold them back, but there was no stopping them. She shifted her head slightly, a minor victory that allowed a sprig of hope to rise within her.

A heavy boot stepped down on her shoulder, pressing down both her stunted mobility and any hope along with it.

"Now, you don't want to be going anywhere, do ya?" A satisfied smile stretched across Harold's ugly face as he leaned over her. Faint light from the nearby fire elongated shadows of his crooked beak nose and ball cap. "We were just gettin' to know one another."

Chapter Eight

Annika

The stench of sweat and grime permeated from the offending foot beside Annika's face. She had managed to turn her head just enough to get a glimpse of the black steel-toed boot that rested on her shoulder, but she immediately regretted moving her nose closer toward the smell.

"Why would either of you want to go anywhere?" Harold drawled, swaying with drink. "Maybe it was the hand of God that brought you here, or maybe it was fate, but if you're gonna survive, I'd recommend you stick around."

"You think threats are going to make me want to stay?"

Harold scoffed. "That's not a threat, lovely. We're the only ones who are gonna survive the end of days."

Annika shifted her gaze from the repugnant boot that still rested on top of her and found the face of the man who held her captive for the second time that day. Shadows danced across his pockmarked face. It might have been the dim light, but his T-shirt appeared to have more stains on it than when she'd first saw him. There was a darkness to his gaze as the flickering of the nearby fire danced across his face, playing tricks with his features.

Engines roared before fading into the distance.

"We're just about to leave. You'll be safe now."

Annika spat toward the offending man's boot. "Are you sure your people didn't just leave you here to rot? I know I'd rather take my chances with the bots."

"Harold!" Annika recognized Frank's voice barking into the night. "What the hell are you doing? The caravan's leaving."

"You won't believe this!" Harold called back. "A gift from the heavens."

Hurried footsteps crunched through the gravel as Frank got closer.

"Damn it, Harold!" Frank said. "What have you done? I've told you, we're not hurting people now."

"I used the stunner," Harold protested. "They're scraped up, but they're okay. Look! She's come back to us!"

Frank's shadow crossed over Annika's line of sight. His broad shoulders, V-shaped figure, and flat head were unmistakable.

"Well, I'll be damned. I never thought I'd see you again. I see you took my advice and ran. And lucky for you, you were led back into the arms of salvation. God works in mysterious ways. Seems as though you were meant to be with us."

Annika shivered. "I'm sure if it were predestined, you wouldn't need to keep taking me against my will."

Frank chuckled. "Sometimes, we don't know what's best for us. The path can be laid out without us knowing it's the right one. Sometimes, we just need a little help following it."

"And what do you know about what's best for me?" Annika flexed her fingers, testing their agility, running them through the coarse gravel beneath her but trying not to disturb it enough to garner attention.

"Dunno," Frank responded. "But clearly you're here for a reason."

Harold's boot pushed down slightly; not enough to be

painful, but enough to let her know he wasn't going to let her move. "Quit squirming," he said coldly.

Movement in the corner of her eye caught Annika's attention. It only took her a moment to grasp what was happening, and she did her best not to draw the men's attention away from her, continuing to wriggle and fight the men as much as she could. She still didn't have her full range of mobility, but she managed to provide enough of a distraction to give her friend the moment she needed.

Suddenly, she felt Harold's weight shift. "Ah, *shit!*"

Harold removed enough pressure from her back for Annika to twist her head to see Becky making a break for it.

The other woman had stayed quiet through their exchange to give herself an opening. Annika breathed a sigh of relief until she saw the glint of the weapon Harold pulled out. Two shots were fired in quick succession.

Annika recoiled at the noise. Combined with Harold's attention being diverted, the motion allowed her to twist enough to break free of his foot.

Annika pushed herself up, but she didn't get far. Frank's hand grabbed her wrist, wrenching it into an unnatural position. She winced, struggling to breathe under the newfound pain.

"Harold!" Frank yelled. "What the hell did I *just* say? We're *not* hurting people! Not if we don't have to."

Harold's face contorted at the scolding. "But she's getting away, Frank!"

"Who gives a shit? We're not kidnappers."

"My ass," Annika scoffed.

Harold reluctantly lowered his weapon.

"This one's come back to us twice," Frank continued, ignoring the retort. "Call it divine reason, but we're meant to help her out. If the other one wants to resign her fate to the bots, it's no skin off my nose."

Annika exhaled. *At least Becky's escaped.* Though the

implications of capture terrified her, providing enough of a distraction for her friend to leave was at least one less thing off Annika's conscience.

But she still had to get to her sister, and Annika would bet the farm that these lowlifes wouldn't care less, even if they knew her true purpose for being out here.

"Load her up," Frank said. "But no funny business! I don't want to hear no more talk about taking advantage of her. Got it? Or there'll be hell to pay. Show some respect and lay off the booze. We're not animals."

Annika squinted, trying to read Frank's expression. He still held her arm in a vicelike grip, dragging her into the adjacent parking lot. The man had at least changed the angle of her arm enough to provide some relief, but she was sure his mammoth fingers would still leave a bruise. Ridiculously, the man seemed to be playing the hero to Harold's villain, but Annika couldn't quite ascertain if it was for real or for show. Perhaps this was a 'good cop, bad cop' routine meant to have her let her guard down. She didn't believe for one moment that Frank was genuine in his concern for her well-being.

A dated pickup truck sat off to one side, near to the flame-filled barrel the terrorists had been huddled around a few minutes earlier. A few sticks of wood still hung over its lip, haphazardly tossed in to fuel the fire. Those sticks would be hot for hours.

A teal green stripe was painted over the otherwise white-bodied pickup. Some of Annika's friends in Saskatchewan had grandparents with vehicles that old. They were still good for driving through the fields when automated machinery couldn't as long as the farmers kept them maintained. Though Annika knew, from talk in the town, that parts for the units were getting harder and harder to come by.

The truck was the sole vehicle left in the lot. She cocked

her head enough to make out a convoy of taillights disappearing into the distance.

Annika could just make out the shadows of the industrial garage that sat behind it—CLARK COUNTY ANTIQUE REPAIRS—a custom mechanic and restoration shop for gasoline-powered vehicles. Though not technically road-legal machines any longer, the Department of Motor Vehicles made exceptions for collectors, and some enthusiasts could skirt the rules if they were smart about it. Other exceptions existed depending on the state. This would have provided a medley of non-sentient machines to choose from.

It seemed a logical place for the anti-automation anarchists to congregate. Their distrust of the bots clearly fueled every action they took, though after the day she'd had, Annika was finding it harder and harder to disagree with their core values. What set them apart was the extreme lengths the anarchists were prepared to go to, to spread their truth.

Seeing as though both men seemed in a talkative mood, Annika decided to keep them talking, in the hope that her own opportunity to abscond would present itself. "Is this your shop or something?" she asked. "Or did you kill the owners and steal their stuff?"

Frank rose to the bait. "One of our members owns it, smart-ass. People sell him their old vehicles when they can't drive them anymore. He's been restoring them for years. Keeping them ready for when the time was right."

"And you just happened to know that there'd be a robot apocalypse this week?"

Frank's grip tightened on Annika's arm, and she successfully refrained from crying out at the pain.

"It's been a long time coming," Frank insisted. "Not just the bots. Our infrastructure has been vulnerable for years. Could be an EMP blast, a hostile nation state hacking into our grid, a nuclear attack—you name it. We're lucky we've made it this long without the world falling apart. Like I said, it's *fate* that brought you to us, lovely. We've been preppin' for something like this for a long time."

Frank tossed Annika over to Harold, who grabbed her left arm just as roughly and pulled her uncomfortably close to his damp, sweaty body. The smell from the man's T-shirt and jeans passed over Annika in waves, turning her stomach to the point where she thought she might vomit what little food she'd eaten in the past twenty-four hours.

As they passed the back of the truck, another sour smell assaulted Annika's nose. Surprisingly, in contrast to her captor's overpowering odor, the scent reminded her of being back on the farm. It took her a moment to spot the jerry cans lining the truck bed.

"Gasoline-powered vehicles, and enough fuel to last a few days. What are you planning?"

"Hun, we have enough fuel to last us *years*. Maybe even longer. This is just going to get us to where we're goin'. Don't worry, though. You'll see once we get there."

"You're going off-grid?" Annika asked.

"If you haven't noticed, we're *all* going off-grid. The power ain't comin' back."

Fear wrapped itself around Annika's throat. Everything Hailey and Terre had talked about on their drive from the city came flooding back. She knew the current national emergency was bad, but it hadn't quite sunk in how depraved the state of the world might become. Never mind what the bots could or couldn't do, if the people didn't have access to power, a few looters in a Walmart warehouse would seem trivial. If people had to deal with their power grid permanently shutting down on top of a robot insurrection ... Annika imagined there would be little hope.

Frank made his way to the driver's side of the pickup, Harold's grip unrelenting. Annika's arm ached from the pressure, but she had one free hand, and the number of men near her had gone from two to one. If she was going to act, it had to be now.

All I need to do is distract him long enough to make a break for it.

A piece of wood sticking out of the flaming barrel hung just within her reach. As they passed, her right hand grabbed the wooden shard. Enough of the stick hung outside of the pit for the wood to be cool enough to grip, but even as her fingers wrapped around the would-be weapon, Annika realized she'd miscalculated.

She heaved with her right arm, but the stick was weighted down by an unseen obstacle on top of it. It scraped and screeched against the metal of the barrel before it broke loose.

Harold reflexively yanked on her left arm, pulling her toward him, and the movement was enough to free the torch from its prison. Annika whipped it around as best she could, sparks catapulting into the night.

But as she attempted to swing, she realized she didn't have enough room to follow through. The searing of hot wood singeing against flesh hissed as Harold instinctively grabbed at the stick swinging toward him.

Annika held back a satisfactory grin as Harold let out a yelp, his hand wrapping around the glowing stick, followed by the stench of burning flesh.

"Why, you little …!" Harold yelled, but he didn't get to finish. The painful distraction caused his grip to falter just enough for Annika to wrestle free. His greasy fingers slipping over her arm before losing it altogether, Annika drove an elbow into his gut, sending the brute doubling over.

A *thud* sounded behind her as the hot stick fell to the ground and Harold let out a winded grunt.

Annika turned and took three steps before the sound of a gunshot penetrated the night sky, causing her to stumble and crouch to the ground. She froze in place, mentally checking her extremities in an instant to determine if the anarchists had shot her.

Only the soreness of her arm from being manhandled and the stiffness in her calves from being on her feet all day betrayed any discomfort. It was only then that she dared to crane her head enough to spot Frank, a pistol held high and pointed above his head, smoke still wafting from its barrel.

"Get … in … the … truck."

Chapter Nine

Terre

Terre realized his mistake as his calls into the night went unanswered. He had exposed their hiding place behind the building.

Dozens of pairs of eyes now locked onto him, and none of them were Annika's. Men and women, their faces hollow and their eyes greedy, were now aware of him. From the looks of their empty arms and empty shopping carts, they had just emerged from the surrounding stores and had turned up empty-handed. The shelves had already been picked clean.

The gaunt, stretched faces of the already malnourished were now terrified, and as Terre stood before them in his blazer, designer jeans, and Oxford style dress shoes, however dirtied, they smelled opportunity.

Nobody moved, but their eyes darted from Terre to the place he had emerged from. Their glassy stares indicated that, if they weren't bold enough to take on the large black man before them, they would scour the area from where he'd emerged as soon as he was out of sight.

Terre suddenly felt more vulnerable than he had in a long

time. The sea of trucker hats and blunt objects was a recipe for unsolicited violence. He had to move.

He took a step back and jumped as he bumped into the soft flesh of a person. Hackles raised, he spun around, poised for action, only to discover that it was Hailey who stood behind him.

"Come on," she said. "We can't stick around, acting like we're lost."

Terre released a breath, placing a hand to his chest to feel the quickened pace of his heart. He shook off the adrenaline spike and motioned back toward the vehicle. "Let's move."

Several of the people in the nearest parking lot had turned their full attention on them. The scavengers slowly made their way forward, judging how the newcomers were going to react, like a cat testing its prey. A few of the men catcalled at Hailey. Terre couldn't quite hear the remarks, but he caught the tone, and knew they were lewd.

The blood within him boiled at the intonation, and the CD-115 blaster weighed heavy against his hip. He wouldn't shoot it at anyone unprovoked, not unless he had no other choice, but its presence provided a sense of protection in case anything should go wrong. But it was a false comfort, and he knew it. The scavengers looting and helping themselves to the store shelves were already desperate, likely armed, and there were a lot of them.

Hailey must have read his thoughts. She placed a warm hand on his skin and shook her head. "Not worth it."

Terre nodded as Hailey led him back toward the SUV. How many of the vultures on the main road would have seen them pull into the alley?

"A gas-powered vehicle in the middle of a power outage will probably attract some unwanted attention," he said.

"If the lights don't come back on," Hailey said, "they won't wait for us to get out in order to take it, either."

If they were going to camp out for the night, Terre knew

they needed to move, either deeper into the residential areas where the looting would hopefully be minimal, or into the outskirts, which would provide its own set of challenges.

Hailey stepped to the side of the SUV, opening the driver's side door and pulling herself in. Terre paused, looking back into the darkness.

Nobody made you her hero.

A gunshot sounded, breaking the otherwise eeriness of the evening. Terre spun around, trying to identify the direction of the shot, but nothing visible had changed.

"Not our concern, Hoffman." Hailey stood on the side of the SUV, her arms holding onto the roll bars above as she called, "Let's get moving!"

Terre's gut roiled as the sound of the gunshot dissipated. Annika was out there, and he had no doubt that, regardless of who had fired that weapon, his newfound friend was in trouble.

Hailey's calls and curses faded behind him as he pushed off in the direction he believed Annika had gone.

In the same direction from which someone had fired the gun.

His pace was brisk. Terre could hear the roar of the vehicle firing up behind him. Apparently, Hailey wasn't going to wait for him to get in.

Terre didn't blame her. Judging by the greed in the eyes of the looters, if the SUV hadn't been hot-wired and stolen by the time they got back, it would likely have been stripped for parts.

Annika and Becky probably hadn't gotten far, though. So, rather than heading back to the vehicle, Terre increased his speed in pursuit.

Hailey pulled the SUV up beside him, the warmth of its exhaust amplifying the heat of the desert evening.

"Terre, we can't be messing around like this. We've got to find somewhere to rest for the night."

Rest. It was all he'd wanted for the past few months—but his mind wouldn't let him.

Hell, who was he kidding? Fredricks, Hailey, even Annika was running him ragged. There would be little rest in the cards for him tonight.

Suddenly, Terre longed for another glass of scotch and the company of the Grand Kawa's robot bartender.

But Annika and Becky were out there somewhere. He had dragged the two women into the desert—it was his fault they were here to begin with.

"Didn't you hear the gunshot?" he asked, not slowing his pace. "I just want to take a look. If we haven't found them within ten minutes, we'll move on without her."

Terre wasn't sure why he'd settled on ten minutes—Annika could be anywhere by now—but he had to offer Hailey something of a bargaining chip. Perhaps the small window would be enough.

The whites of Hailey's eyes glistened as she rolled them. "*Fine.* Ten minutes. Get in, at least. We'll cover more ground."

Terre eyed her suspiciously at the sudden change in tune. Had the tactic actually worked? Or maybe she just didn't believe they'd find Annika in such a short amount of time, or that ten minutes less sleep just wouldn't matter. Either way, Terre reluctantly grabbed onto the side of the SUV and pulled himself in.

Terre pointed forward, past the stretch of an alley where the headlights touched. "They couldn't have gone far, and the gunshot came from that way. We might as well start there."

"Chasing gunshots in the dark isn't what I'd call a smart plan, Hoffman."

"It's no coincidence that shot was so close. Or that it came from the direction in which they were headed."

The SUV rolled slowly forward, past darkened warehouses, custom shops, and storage units, until their surroundings became increasingly residential. They were going to need to make the call soon as to whether to turn onto the 515 freeway or not, and once they were on that path, it would be more difficult to find a place to stay for the night. That was *if* they could make any headway through the barricades of vehicles, and who knew what kind of mayhem hundreds of cars coming to a halt on that roadway would have caused?

Either way, time was running out. Terre knew Hailey would stick to the ten-minute window he had offered. After that, Annika and Becky would be on their own.

The SUV continued to wind through parking lots and over sidewalks. There weren't many options unless they wanted to take the vehicle completely into the residential areas, and if Annika had cut through backyards and alleys, their hope of finding her was next to none.

The further they went, the fewer people they saw, and the more unlikely that Annika and Becky would have ventured so far in the short time they'd been separated. Raiders-turned-to-residents now hid in their homes, afraid their supplies might be the next to be pillaged.

The tires of the SUV crunched as it went, rolling over dry dirt and gravel, as well as refuse fleeing survivors had cast aside.

Hailey slammed on the brakes, wrenching Terre from his thoughts. A ghost stood on the road before them; a woman basked in the bright white headlights of the SUV. Terre had to blink a few times before recognition registered. Becky had her arms wrapped around herself.

Sweat and tears had washed away Becky's mascara long ago, but her puffy eyes betrayed she had been crying. Terre could feel the intensity of his pulse pounding against the seatbelt strapped over his chest. He licked his lips as all moisture disappeared from his palate. Whatever the reason for Becky's tears, Annika was noticeably absent, and his mind soared into worst-case scenarios.

Before Terre could react, Hailey was already out of the car, an arm wrapped around the shivering woman, who looked as though she had narrowly escaped death. Loyal to a fault, the woman had run alongside Annika until she was past the point of exhaustion, and then she'd got up and ran some more. Terre marveled at the woman's tenacity and realized he could only wish for someone who would be as quick to jump to his aid. His wife Cara had lived on a military base for *three years* to support him, but Terre wasn't sure her dedication to him in any way rivaled Becky's toward Annika. True friendship was something that seemed to be scarce.

Hailey helped Becky into the back seat of the SUV. With the top down, the vehicle offered little warmth on its own, but Hailey stepped to the back, pulled out what must have been an emergency blanket, and wrapped it around the newcomer.

"Are you okay?" she asked.

Becky shivered in the backseat, her eyes downcast, unfocused. "They've got Anni."

Terre's pulse kicked up about ten notches. "*Who* has her?"

Becky shook her head, her eyes still locked on the floor of the vehicle. "I don't know who they were, but she seemed to recognize them. I got away, but we need to find her. They were talking about taking us out into the desert. I don't know what they have planned, but it didn't sound good. Whatever's happening, with the cars and the bots, I think they were expecting it somehow. They had a bunch of gas-powered vehicles and supplies."

Hailey didn't waste any time in shifting the SUV into drive. "Can you tell us where they are?"

Becky pointed to a set of tire tracks on the side of the road that led into a large open space, just off the corner of the exit to the 515 freeway. "Follow that path."

Two marks lined an empty field leading north of the city,

away from the freeway and toward the mountains. The SUV shuddered as Hailey jumped the curb and stomped down on the gas. All previous thoughts of preserving fuel were now behind them.

Terre held his breath as they passed the last of the industrial area. A half-mile down the trail, a small fire appeared, casting shadows in the barrel that contained it. Beyond it, a pair of taillights faded into darkness.

Chapter Ten

Annika

The old Ford pickup creaked over every bump and dip as it raced over the back trails of the Las Vegas city limits. Frank seemed adept at avoiding the looters, turning and weaving as if on a predetermined path. Well-manicured lawns and cookie-cutter homes stood tall and proud as the back alleys opened briefly into suburbia, venturing past several side streets and a golf course.

Nobody was out and about, though Annika could make out curtains slightly pulled back as residents sought to determine the source of the gasoline engine that roared through the eeriness of the evening.

Only a few half-constructed homes marked the boundary between the city and the Mojave Desert beyond. Annika braced herself as the Ford hopped a curb onto a rocky lot and then swerved onto some rarely traveled back road that led into the desert.

The clock on the dash ticked slowly as the night wore on. The only thing providing Annika with any comfort was that the men beside her remained relatively silent. She didn't have to endure their small talk or uncomfortable pickup lines.

She tried not to stare at the clock, also avoiding thoughts

about what kind of middle of the desert hell they were taking her to, or whether it would be the last place she ever saw.

What plagued Annika's thoughts instead was the fact that every mile of desert they crossed was another mile further from Cheyenne. They were headed north, in the opposite direction from where she needed to go, and every minute of driving was that much more running she'd have to do once she escaped.

Because she *would* escape. Annika gritted her teeth as they bumped along the trail. She would either break free or she would die trying, but she wouldn't rest until her sister was back with her. Until her sister was safe. That was paramount. Nothing else mattered.

The inside of the truck's cabin was dank and musty. Dust had swept through the vents for nearly a century, and though the seating and dashboard had all been meticulously cleaned and restored, it was as though the ventilation system hadn't received the same sort of treatment. Or perhaps the tired filtration units that fitted the old intake couldn't keep up with the amount of dust displaced by the sand and grit the desert afforded.

It didn't help that the two men sat on either side of Annika stank of sweat and bourbon. At least one of them had smoked a cigar at some point recently, and smoke from the burning stogie had latched itself onto their clothes and held on, filling the truck with its stench. Annika grew sick from the stench, her stomach already nauseous from being tasered earlier in the evening. Waves of an unsettled stomach passed through her, and for a while, it was touch and go whether she would lose her lunch before their trip ended.

It didn't help that she hadn't eaten anything since lunch—nothing but the dried-out protein bar Terre had given her back at the hotel. The realization made Annika's stomach growl, but the stench tampered the hunger as bile fought to stay down.

Red brake lights illuminated not too far ahead of them, the rest of the terrorists' companions leading the way into the unknown.

"You're just going to live in the desert mountains?" Annika asked, breaking the silence as she shifted uncomfortably on the truck's bench. The two criminals had shoved her into the middle of the cab, something Harold seemed to enjoy far too much. His hand roamed freely under the guise of adjusting his seatbelt. "Eat scorpions and snakes until the end of days passes?"

Annika shuffled as much as she could, but Harold held a pistol to her ribs to ensure she got the hint that escape wasn't an option. As they'd entered the truck earlier, she'd noticed Harold had tossed another weapon in the glove compartment. There were probably more stashed away that the two men could grab in an emergency.

Annika cursed herself again for being so foolhardy; for thinking she could head out into the desert and find Cheyenne on her own. If she had just thought things through rationally, she'd be holed up with Terre, Hailey, and Becky somewhere right now, instead of back with the pervert terrorists on their way to their orgy campsite.

"We'll stay in the desert tonight." Frank's eyes drifted skyward through the windshield, his confident demeanor shifting every time a light from a jet or drone flew by. "Let things cool down. In the morning, we head west."

Dozens of pinpoints of lights flew above them, headed toward the city. Annika guessed, whatever their purpose, they weren't benevolent. The three passengers instinctively ducked, even though the size of the pinpricks revealed they were miles above them. These weren't the orbs she had seen earlier; the ones Terre had called the Onyx. Nor were they standard military UAVs. These were smaller, flying in a uniformed pattern across the sky. She shuddered at what it might mean for the city's survivors, but she had her own problems to worry about.

"You think you're going to get away with what you've done?" she asked defiantly, referring to the explosions along the Strip. "Every Homeland Security agent in the country is going to be after you."

"Sis," Frank said, his eyes still on the lights flying overhead, "I don't think you realize the magnitude of what's happened tonight. Soon, there ain't goin' to be a homeland to secure. The Feds created a system that could have been used to make our lives better. You know what they did with it? The first two things we did with this godforsaken tech? We created war machines and manipulated the stock market." He held up two fingers in succession to emphasize his point. "We could have fed the entire planet, stopped global warming, ended just about every ailment out there. Did you know there's tech out there that could let you live forever? Instead, we kill each other. People have become the tool of their tools. You're witnessing the end."

"People are more resilient than you think."

"*Hah!* You saw those people back in the city? They look *resilient* to you? They'll pick the shelves bare by tomorrow morning, if they haven't already. And then what? How long do you think they'll stay good and decent people? A *week*, tops. Almost nobody knows how to live without tech. Where do you think they're goin' to get food from? Hungry people are desperate people. Ain't nobody who won't be desperate after tonight. We ain't comin' back from this one."

"Then why did you plant the bombs at the hotels? Why add to people's misery?"

"That wasn't the plan. We were too late," Frank said, shaking his head. "We were trying to warn them. You think people would've clued in after San Fran. We should have shut down those military bots then, but the government likes to think they're on an equal playing field with God. The scientists and the corporations have been playing God unchecked for years. Now all we can do is look out for ourselves. Try to ensure the bots don't enslave us all. These people"—Frank waved to the vehicles a few hundred yards ahead of them—"we like to call ourselves the Robot Resistance. We know how to survive. We know how to hunt; how to fish; how to find clean water. To survive without tech. You're one of the lucky ones. God chose you to come with us."

"Don't you think God would give me a say in where I should go?"

"God works in mysterious ways," Frank answered. "You never know what your purpose will be until this life is all said and done."

Annika resisted the urge to roll her eyes. "So, now what? You go to your hidey-hole in the mountains and wait for the rest of humanity to burn?"

"We do what we've always done," he replied. "We sabotage, attack, and deface the bots. We defend humanity."

Annika scoffed. Inwardly, though, she couldn't help but think Frank might have a point. After all, it was because of AI that her parents had died. It was because of a bot that her sister was missing. In their earlier conversation, it had sounded as though Terre himself had questioned why the military wasn't striking against the bots that currently flew above the city. She had seen very few units built like Ember, but apparently there were at least hundreds, maybe *thousands*, of Sentinels built for war. More killing machines than guardians—and the result was the machines had turned on them all.

But be that as it may, the anarchists' actions were clearly misdirected. And Cheyenne was still missing. No matter how much sense her kidnappers were beginning to make, she needed to escape. She needed to find her sister.

Moonlight painted the mountains in the distance. Under

any other circumstances, Annika would have marveled at the beauty of the landscape; instead, she shuddered at the hellscape the terrorists had trapped her in. Her mind raced to find an escape, but the men on either side of her and the gun embedded in her ribs weren't offering her any promises.

They have to sleep sometime. Maybe I'll have the chance to escape then.

"Boss?" Harold said. "We're being followed."

"I see 'em," Frank said, his eyes flicking to and from the rearview mirror.

Annika couldn't help but steal a glance for herself. Through the dust their own pickup was kicking up, she instantly recognized the shape of Hailey's SUV. The headlights were dimmed, but the glow of moonlight outlined the frame perfectly.

Despite her best efforts, the two agents hadn't abandoned her after all.

Chapter Eleven

Terre

Terre had watched Interstate 515 disappear in the rearview mirror as they pursued Annika and her captors. Hailey's driving was astounding, taking them over rocks and shrubs as they crossed the vacant lot and into the wilds of the desert that sat just outside the city limits. After crawling along Tropicana Avenue, it now felt as though they were flying.

Hailey had put as much distance as she could between the truck and themselves without losing them. The SUV had traveled in darkness for most of their pursuit, which had worked well enough through the vacant lots and along the side streets as they'd wound their way through suburbia, but things had become a little more complicated once they'd passed the golf course and rolled off-road through brush and rocky terrain.

Branches screeched against the door of the SUV, and desert rocks, each seemingly larger than the last, knocked about beneath them, threatening to pop a tire with their sharp edges. Sand from their pursuit vehicle kicked into their faces. With the top of the SUV missing, every bit of dust settled on top of them. Every inch of Terre itched with grit and dirt, and there was sand in his hair and in his teeth. He was sure some had even made its way into his underwear. It made the pursuit that much more unbearable.

"I'm going to have to turn on the headlights," Hailey said.

"Can't you just follow the taillights?" Terre asked as he hung onto the side of his door for support. "There's no way we're going to stay hidden if you do that."

"It won't matter if we get caught up on a cactus! Brace yourselves, everyone! We don't know if they're going to start shooting."

Terre gripped his CD-115 but refrained from uttering the curses running through his head. He braced himself, his knuckles white around the weapon's grip.

Becky ducked in the back seat as best she could, her hands resting behind her neck as if the act would provide any additional protection.

Headlights instantly lit the terrain before them, providing barely enough time for Hailey to steer around a boulder in their path. Terre braced himself against the car door as the SUV swerved, his hand preoccupied with his blaster.

"We've lost any element of surprise," he said. "We're going to have to overtake them."

Hailey nodded to their pursuit. "I don't think we'll have to worry about that."

Brake lights turned the desert sand bright red as the Ford pickup slowed to a halt, kicking up dust in its wake.

Two men opened the truck doors and got out of either side, their husky features illuminated by the eerie red glow of the taillights. A woman still sat inside the cab, turning in her seat, twisting to get a better view, but not moving to exit the vehicle.

Annika.

Terre couldn't tell if she was being restrained or if she

was simply too terrified to move, but knowing Annika for the short time he had, he knew that if she was capable, she'd flee the vehicle the first moment she sensed an opportunity to do so.

Unless she's injured. Terre shook off the thought. *One problem at a time.*

The two men moved, treading lightly, as though carefully judging each step they took toward the newcomers. The men held their pistols conspicuously, though neither of them directed their weapons at their pursuers.

A lot of show, Terre thought. *They want us to know they won't be afraid to shoot.*

Terre and Hailey held steady in their seats. Becky squirmed in the back, shaking the vehicle momentarily before she settled into a position where she could watch.

The men's faces were cast in shadow until they inched closer and caught the beams of light, illuminating their identities. One had a distinctive white ball cap, smudged now with desert dust and sweat, and a T-shirt, equally stained. The other man was muscular and more put together, his red T-shirt was fitted and, comparatively, could have been freshly laundered.

Terre's jaw dropped.

"You've got to be shitting me!" The thought spilled out, though Terre kept his voice low enough that he didn't think anyone outside the vehicle would have heard.

"What is it?" Hailey answered, her brow furrowed and her hands never leaving the steering wheel. "You know these clowns?"

Terre shook his head. "I was hoping you could tell me. These two were responsible for the Grand Kawa bombing just before you picked me up."

Hailey's eyes didn't leave the pickup in front of them. "Why don't you fill me in?"

"Seriously?" Terre asked. "Explosives blowing out the

windows of the top floors of all the casinos? You didn't notice?"

"Nice one, smart-ass," she said. "How do *you* know them?"

"They'd already kidnapped Annika once," Terre replied. "Held her hostage in the hotel while you were out fighting bots."

"And here I was thinking you'd let me have all the fun. You've been dealing with some hardcore anti-tech anarchists."

"Do you know who they are?"

"The only organization crazy enough to blow devices along the Strip would be the Robot Resistance." Hailey clenched her jaw. "The Agency's been tracking them for months."

"Tracking them for months, but no intel they were planning to wreak havoc on the Las Vegas Strip?"

"They're a small group of extremists that have been overly vocal about their opposition to AI. I haven't been on their detail, so I don't know any specifics about what was or wasn't known." Hailey scoffed as she pushed a dark strand of hair off her face. "All I know is, until tonight, they've been relatively peaceful. Staging protests, live stints on social media, damaging AI units and self-driving cars ... but it's mostly been clickbait. Just another group refusing to acknowledge the necessary future. But, as of late, they've grown their numbers significantly. With that, I suppose it's become harder to reign in the fringes of the group."

"There are millions of disgruntled people who have lost their jobs to automation. It was bound to happen at some point."

"You either lead, follow, or get the hell outta the way. The cell might not be happy to follow, but get off the grid and take your conspiracy theories with you."

Terre lifted an eyebrow. "Conspiracy theories? After today? *Really?*"

"We don't have time for this." Hailey nodded to the men, who were just about beside the SUV. "So, they know who you are?"

"No," Terre replied. "I followed them to the room in order to rescue Annika. But fortunately, they never saw me."

"Is there a reason you're following us?" the athletic man behind the truck called over the hum of their engine.

"Kill the engine," Terre said to Hailey.

Hailey complied as Terre exited the SUV.

"We seem to be a little lost," he said, both hands in the air. "Those bots got us turned around. We saw your taillights and figured you knew something we didn't. Trying to find our way back to the freeway."

"Freeway's behind you," Muscles replied. "But you knew that already. What are you really after?"

Terre paused, considering his options; considering if there would be any reasoning with the two men stood in front of them. Two men involved in the largest terrorist plot in recent memory. A plot that, had it not occurred on the same day as a robot uprising, would have set in motion its own series of chaotic events.

"You've got someone who's important to us. We're taking her back."

Might as well lay our cards on the table. It was either that or start shooting, and Terre could only imagine how poorly that plan would go.

"I'm sorry, can't help you there. It's no longer up to me. Fate's seen to it that she survives what's coming."

"And what's that?" Terre replied.

"Extinction." The man stated the word flatly and without hesitation. "Move on, man. Hide in the mountains if you can. Like I said, freeway's behind you. Don't do something you'll regret."

Terre froze. He wasn't about to let these two whack jobs

take Annika with them for whatever bizarre purposes they had in mind, but he didn't want to make things worse.

"I said, move on!" The burly man held up a shotgun as he motioned with it for them to turn around.

"Easy now!" Terre said. "I'm sure we can work something out."

"There ain't *nothin'* to work out! Either get goin' or regret it. Ain't nobody gonna be the wiser if we bury you out here."

Terre risked studying the back of their vehicle for a moment, trying his best to assess Annika's condition. The man in the ball cap followed Terre's gaze and pushed forward, weapon in hand.

Terre knew one thing for certain: if Annika left with that truck, it'd be the last time he saw her.

He let out a sigh. It was the last thing he wanted to do, but he saw no other option.

With reflexes that surprised even him, Terre pulled out his CD-115 and fired at the man in the ball cap, before diving back toward the SUV. The shot went wide, the weapon's beam kicking up dirt as it slammed into the ground behind its target.

"Terre! *What the hell?*" Hailey screamed, ducking for cover. "Are you crazy?"

Hailey ducked into the driver's seat and pulled out her own weapon.

Shots were fired back at the SUV, pinging against its frame.

Terre lifted his blaster. He knew his aim was shit, so he focused his efforts on drawing the armed man away from the truck. Perhaps Hailey could find a way to make a run for it. Shots from the CD-115 ricocheted off the pickup truck's frame, burning marks into its tailgate, but Terre didn't believe he was doing any actual damage.

"Careful!" Becky cried from the back seat. "You're going to hit Anni!"

Terre took another look at the scorch marks, and then at the truck's interior. Annika had ducked down, but the top of her head was still visible. He'd been lucky the blaster fire hadn't shattered the rear window.

"Aw, hell no!" Ball Cap aimed back at Terre and pulled the trigger.

Terre had just maneuvered to fire a shot and didn't have enough time to react. He lunged to the ground as the deafening discharge roared through the air. A piercing pain struck his left shoulder, just as his right one hit the ground.

Terre grimaced as he pushed himself off the dirt. His left arm was suddenly unable to bear weight, so his right arm needed to do the lifting. He sat, lifted his weapon, and fired twice at the pickup truck, the kickback sending stars through his vision as his shoulder screamed in agony.

A yelp and a deep grunt told Terre his shot had struck true. Two more blaster shots followed. A black cloud circled his vision, pulsing with the pain in his shoulder, and he bit back the overwhelming agony that ripped through his side.

"Stupid bitch!" Ball Cap yelled.

Footsteps. Sobs. Red taillights faded. Were they getting away?

Nope. I'm blacking out.

Chapter Twelve

Annika

With both Harold and Frank distracted, Annika saw her one opportunity for escape. There wouldn't be much time to make her move, and if she made it too soon, she'd be putting herself in harm's way.

Worse than that, she'd also be putting Becky at risk.

Once she was convinced Terre and Hailey had distracted her two captors, she opened the glove compartment, grabbed the handgun Harold had stashed there, and waited for her opportunity to strike.

She peered over her shoulder toward her would-be rescuers.

The entire truck erupted with energy as blaster fire struck its backside, showering the truck bed with sparks.

Annika swore and hit the floor, terrified the shots would miss their mark and strike her through the back window. Whatever had possessed Terre to start shooting was beyond her, but it might just have been the distraction she was looking for.

She stuck her head out of the passenger side door just in time to see Harold lift his weapon and return fire. The explosive noise caused Annika to slip and tumble from the truck and onto the ground below.

Annika lifted a hand to block out some of the blinding glare from the SUV's headlights, but their brilliance wasn't enough to conceal Terre collapsing as the discharged bullet made impact. A final shot from Terre's ray gun fired waywardly.

Annika didn't hesitate. In one fluid movement, she rolled across the ground, found a position where she could take a stand, and squeezed the trigger of the handgun, managing three quick shots, all directed at Harold.

Harold collapsed to the ground with a *thud*. Lifeless.

"Stupid bitch!" Frank yelled from the other side of the vehicle. But it was too late. Blaster fire landed true on the man's chest, sending him flailing. There was a light *clunk* as his weapon struck the ground, shortly followed by the *thud* of its owner.

Hailey lowered her ray gun, the lights from its display panel making following its motion easy.

Annika's legs shook as she stumbled toward the SUV, adrenaline fleeing her body. The coolness of the evening slapped against her skin, chilling the sweat that clung to her back from being pressed against the truck's nylon seat.

Her gaze went from Hailey over to Terre, a heap on the ground, and her breath caught in her chest. She had seen Terre go down, but in the throes of everything, the man's condition hadn't registered.

The aftermath of the skirmish was sprawled out over the desert sand, and the reality of Annika's actions overcame her. Two men lay dead on the earth, and one more lay wounded. Her gut ached, as though someone had punched it, and her lungs burned, as though she were breathing flames instead of air. Each breath a struggle as her mind tried to come to terms with her actions. She willed her legs to have strength; willed her body to cooperate even though it wanted to collapse under its own weight. Pins and needles coursed through her legs, but she forced them to stand; forced them to stumble toward the stranger who had saved her life more than once in the past twenty-four hours.

Annika let out a gasp as she tried to catch her breath. It came out as a squeak instead. "I'm sorry! I'm so, so sorry, Terre!"

"*Shh!*" Becky said as she came up beside her, grabbing Annika's hands in her own. "This isn't your fault! You didn't cause this."

"I did! I ..." Annika struggled to find the words as her mind raced past all the accusations. "I shot a man!"

You killed him. You nearly killed Terre. Dead—because of me.

"Stop, Anni!" Becky grabbed her and pulled her close. "Those men are the ones who did this. He would have killed you if you didn't shoot him first! It's their fault Terre's hurt. Not yours!"

Annika didn't believe her, but the comfort of her friend's embrace allowed her to slow her breathing. Terre lay on the ground. She needed to focus; needed to help.

Becky was already there before Annika could move, removing Terre's suit jacket and placing her delicate hands over the wound. The vehicle's headlights illuminated the red blood staining Terre's dress shirt.

Terre's eyes glossed over, blood pooling beneath him.

"Ah, *shit!* No, Terre ... Stay with us!" Becky cursed. She ripped his shirt off, trying to control the flow of blood as best she could.

Annika stared at Terre's physique—she'd hardly expected a computer programmer to be incredibly fit, the lines of his chest and abdomen defined—but she pushed the thought aside. They had to focus on the problem at hand—keeping the man alive.

Hailey rushed over from the back of the SUV, carrying a gallon-sized jug of water that had been stashed in the back.

"It's a good thing you came well prepared," Annika said, taking the jug and twisting the cap.

"Prepared enough for the end of the world," Hailey replied. She put her hands on her hips rather nonchalantly, considering her colleague was dying before them.

Annika had no time to analyze the other woman's thought process. She brought the jug to Terre and poured it over his dark skin as Becky wiped the wound clean with the unsullied portion of Terre's shirt. The blood diluted in the water, running off in a light pink onto the dirt below them, mixing with the rest of the blood beneath him.

Annika blinked as the water went from pink to clear. Pockmarks where the bullet spray would have hit the man appeared to be dry and healed over, as though he had been shot years ago, rather than minutes.

Annika watched as Becky dabbed where the larger wound had been moments before. To her surprise, the blood had completely stopped flowing. Annika stopped cold. Becky wiped the last of the bloody wound—except there was no wound. There wasn't even a mark where the bullet had struck him.

"What's happening?" Becky asked. "Why has the bleeding stopped?" She touched the spot where the wound had been moments before, rubbing her fingers across Terre's chest as if she couldn't believe her eyes.

Annika, similarly uncertain, couldn't help but put a hand to Terre's skin. It was hot—burning hot, as though he had a severe fever—but the skin was smooth. There was no evident trace of the gunshot wound. She would have questioned whether Terre had even been shot at all, had she not witnessed it with her own eyes or without the man's bloody shirt and muddied soil below him telling a different story.

"Nanobots." Hailey had grabbed an armful of supplies from the terrorists' truck and was loading them into the back of their SUV; blankets, but also weapons and other supplies. "He'll be fine. Load him into the back seat."

Annika squinted as her eyes tried to focus on the woman loading up the back of the vehicle. Was she serious? "Nanobots? Like, inside of him?"

"Yeah, he's full of them. The military injected him after his base in Guam was attacked."

"So, you're saying he's bulletproof? Those guys couldn't have hurt him?"

"Don't be ridiculous." Hailey closed the back of the SUV. "If they had hit his heart or head, he'd be dead. Do you need a hand lifting him?"

Annika stood, her face still contorted. "I thought nanobot tech was still experimental? You're telling me thousands of tiny robots swimming inside him healed a bullet wound?"

"Seems like you've figured it out. And they *are* experimental. Consider them a *perk*"— Hailey lifted her hand to make air quotes—"of working for the government. But, seriously, I don't have time to write you a paper about it. Terre will be fine, but he's going to need rest. We can't wait for the rest of the Robot Resistance to realize dumb and dumber aren't behind them any longer. Let's move."

Annika shared a doubtful glance with Becky, whose wide eyes confirmed that whatever they had just witnessed was nothing short of miraculous, despite Hailey's dismissiveness. Becky grabbed a blanket from the back of the SUV and wrapped it around Terre's naked torso. She then reached down and lifted the man, beneath his armpits, gesturing for Annika to take his feet.

Between the two of them, they managed to lift him into the vehicle and lay him across the back seat.

"You hold on to him," Annika said. "I'll grab shotgun."

Becky nodded as she climbed into the vehicle, placing the man's head and shoulders on her lap while she did her best to gracefully hold on to him.

Annika quietly sat next to Hailey, a little apprehensive about what the other woman might say about her failed attempt to find Cheyenne without their help. Annika's heart hung heavy as the SUV turned a full one-eighty and began traversing the terrain that would lead them back to where they'd started. Her cheeks burned as she looked back at Terre. His breathing was steady and deep.

If they had hit his heart, he'd be dead.

The bullet spray couldn't have been more than an inch or two from killing him outright. Things could have gone worse. *So much* worse. And despite what Becky claimed, it *was* her fault.

Terre didn't have to come looking for them, but he had. Why? Annika hadn't asked for anything from this complete stranger, yet he seemed intent on going out of his way to save her ass. Risking his own mission to get her out of harm's way.

And because of her, he'd almost died. She shook her head.

Annika took a deep breath. This was no time for what-ifs. The important thing was that he *had* come after them; that she and Becky had escaped. Terre was okay, and because of him, they would be able to go after Cheyenne. She hoped, at least.

"So, what now?" Annika said tentatively, studying Hailey's face for disappointment. She breathed a sigh of relief when she found none.

"Same as before. We find a place to hole up for the night," Hailey said. "Those nanos may have saved Terre from the bullet wound, but his body will still need to rest to deal with the trauma. In the morning, we need to track down his mark."

"His mark? The programmer?"

"Yep, that's the one."

As much as Annika was uncertain about Terre, Hailey remained the more enigmatic mystery. Terre had seemed surprised by her role in everything that had transpired over the course of the day, and they hadn't seen eye to eye about what to do about the man they were looking for.

Despite the help of the two agents, Annika had meant what she'd said before: she didn't give a damn about their target. She didn't care about anything other than finding her sister.

"So, we're still heading out to the Dam? We can still find Cheyenne and Terre's friend, and hopefully put a stop to this."

"Finding your sister isn't our priority," Hailey replied pointedly. "If you come across her, great—but we've got bigger things to worry about. I don't know what Terre's obsession is with saving your ass, but if we don't get to Klein in time, everything we've worked for will be lost."

Annika felt panic building in her chest. Her breathing quickened as she shot a worried glance at the back seat to judge Becky's reaction. Her friend was gazing out of the vehicle into the night, as if she wasn't paying attention.

"The whole reason I'm here is because you said my sister was probably headed in the same direction, out toward the Dam. But you have no intention of helping her once we're there?"

"We'll take you out there, but I can't make any promises past that. Terre might be willing to jump for you, honey, but I'm only here for one reason. I won't let anything else get in my way."

"Then why are you helping me at all? Why did you come back for me?"

Hailey smiled disdainfully. "Believe me, it wasn't my idea. Despite you being a pain in the ass diversion, Terre seems to think he's your hero. I humored him this time, but trust me, if you take off again, we're *not* going after you. If you want to come with us in the morning, we still have enough seats for you. But if you're not okay with how we're running things, I suggest you two take off before he wakes up. I'll take you as far as I'm going tonight."

If Annika had proved anything to herself over the course of the day, it was that she only made a mess of things when trying to go it alone. She was ill-equipped to handle the desert, and prone to finding those who were up to no good. She was no stranger to the wilderness, no stranger to hiking, but she was out of her depth in the wilds of Nevada, and there were apparently more nefarious forces standing in her way than she'd bargained for.

And she hadn't even come across another bot yet.

The realization struck her that, despite her best intentions, she was floundering in a foreign land. For nearly as long as she could remember, Annika had been the one responsible for her little family. The one who kept them together. The one who did what was necessary.

None of that mattered now.

She was powerless against it all. Her independence had been stripped from her. Just like how fate had forced her to accept the help of Ember to keep Cheyenne, Annika now relied on others to get her back. The only choice she had was to take the assistance of these strangers who had offered it. Even if it was begrudgingly.

The SUV bounced along the rocky desert soil, the night air blowing through her hair. At any other time, it would be a liberating experience, but tonight, she felt trapped. Annika was at the mercy of events she had no control over, just like when she was a teenager. The desert surrounding her might as well have been up in flames. The bots had split apart her family once again, and Annika didn't know if she'd be able to bring the pieces back together.

Once again, she felt helpless against the forces working to drive them apart.

Chapter Thirteen

Terre

Wisps of conversation bounced around Terre as consciousness came and went. Flashes of pain encompassed his waking moments. Dreams haunted him, where death and destruction awaited him: bots firing on his family, his house in Guam only a hole in the ground; beams of blaster fire erupting on casino floors; hundreds of automated vehicles driving down the freeway, bowling over innocent victims in their path. The most vivid showed K leading an army of bots across the desert plain, holding a fictional flag in front of the mechanized units made of metal and synthetic flesh. The earth quaked beneath the power of their force, each footstep vibrating through his core and reminding Terre of the failure he truly was.

Each time he returned to consciousness was a relief, but Terre couldn't hold the nightmarish scenes at bay for long, and soon his eyes would close and the next series of images would taunt him, reminding him he was as powerless to stop them as he had been to save Las Vegas; as he had been to save his wife and daughter.

More scenes were filled with Annika, searching for her faceless sister. His hallucinations refused to show the face of the girl he had yet to meet, just as they refused to show them achieving a successful rescue. At each turn, they came up empty-handed. Cheyenne was little more than a phantom, neither living nor dead, lost in the limbo of dream as others died around them.

And all the while K watched in the distance, laughing maniacally, his wild, scraggily black hair unkept and feral.

In each of the dreams, Terre's arm was missing. He couldn't decipher if any of what he was seeing was real or not, but a memory tickled each scene regarding his shoulder. He had been shot. The one thought was constant, the pain ever present. Each time he looked down at his arm, it was a bionic appendage. Not truly his. Cold, metallic; separate from who he truly was.

An exact replica of the Sentinels he was attempting to avoid.

It was morning before he woke.

In the darkness, it took him moments to make out if he were truly awake or if it was another dream, and destruction might be wrought down on them at any moment.

His skin itched with the work of the nanos in his system. Terre couldn't help but scratch his abdomen to relieve the discomfort, then his hands worked their way to his shoulder. The smooth sensation of his skin reassured him; actual skin, not metal or silicon. The memory of the bionic arm in his dream was like an icy blast of water to the face, bringing him to full alertness.

"Glad to see you're alive."

The smooth persona Hailey had adopted when Terre had first met her at the bar of the Grand Kawa Resort was all but gone. It had quickly dissipated after the woman had picked up him and the two other women in her SUV. Behind the manicure and stylized hair, this Hailey was rough around the edges, no-nonsense, determined, with a goal locked in a steel trap that nobody would dissuade her from.

She was the calculated agent the Agency had trained her to be.

Terre allowed his eyes to adapt to the dim room. The sun was still down, and light from the full moon outside cast shadows against the white walls, filling the room of wherever he had been dragged to with muted white light.

"I shouldn't be," he replied. His fingers lingered on his shoulder. "Take it I was shot?"

"Oh, you were shot all right," Hailey responded. Terre swore he spotted an amused glint in her eye. "A couple inches over, he would have hit your heart. No amount of nanos would have been able to fix that."

Terre followed the hardwood flooring to a half-finished wall. Drywall had been installed, but it was only taped, unfinished and unpainted. The room's windows still had plastic surrounding them. Across the small room lay Annika and Becky, curled up against the side of the wall with blankets the women must have brought in from the SUV.

"How long have I been out for?"

Terre didn't really need to ask. A hint of yellow light was breaking on the horizon, competing with the moonlight in the final hours of twilight. The sun would come up soon, but in the remnants of his wild dreams, Terre had worried the injury would knock him out for more than a day. Now he was conscious, he realized he knew better; there was no way Hailey would have waited around that long. She would have gone after Kristopher alone at the first sign of delay.

"We'll be heading out soon," Hailey replied as she leaned against an empty window, her gaze lost in the distance.

Terre's hand unconsciously lingered on his chest. It was only then he realized he wasn't wearing a shirt.

"Where are my clothes?" he asked, searching the nearby floor for his belongings.

"Caked with blood," Hailey responded. "I think Becky tossed them somewhere along the way. But if you search the duffel bag in the corner, you might find something in there. Something from one of your Resistance buddies. It looks like they were on the move to a prearranged location."

Terre didn't waste time rifling through the bag, pulling out an oversized flannel button-down shirt and wrapping it around his frame. He shivered at the grisly implication of Hailey's possession of the bag.

"I'm guessing you killed them?"

His voice felt cold as Terre uttered the words, but there was no love lost on the two terrorists. He'd heard the derogatory comments one of the men had made as he held Annika in the stairwell at the Kawa. And that was before they blew the rooms out of a dozen hotels on the Strip. Still, part of him felt callous casually discussing their deaths while wearing one of their shirts.

"Annika took out the one who shot you. Took him out before he could fire another round. I hit the second one before he could turn on her."

Terre had seen his fair share of death in the past few months, but this was the closest he'd come to being part of the reason for it. He tried to push the implications from his mind.

"Hey," Hailey said, her voice softening for the first time since they'd left the Kawa. Empathy momentarily finding a home in her dark brown eyes. "Killing isn't something I enjoy, but sometimes it's necessary."

Terre sighed. He realized the implications of what would have happened if they hadn't acted. His shoulder might have healed, but he still felt the soreness the bullet had left behind.

"What is this place?" His voice came out gruff, dry from the desert air and a night of his body recuperating. He dug around further in the duffel bag and pulled out a bottle of water.

"A new construction in the suburbs of Vegas," Hailey

answered. "Somewhere removed enough from the looting and others looking for a place to stay."

Terre found his gaze drifting out the window. They were at the base of a hill, just high enough to see the Strip in the distance, the outline of the towers and attractions emerging as first light made its appearance.

Above the city, hundreds of lights hovered. As he watched, a dozen dropped from the air and ignited over the homes below.

"Micro drones."

Terre had seen their development and testing at the base in Guam, but he'd never seen them in use outside of the testing facility. Meant to drive the enemy out of hiding, the drones themselves were no more than a foot or two wide. Sent in by the hundreds, it was a one-way deployment; the units would steer themselves to a strategic location and explode upon impact.

"They've been detonating over the residential area all night," Hailey stated, her long nails ticking against the windowsill. "Driving people from their homes, ensuring they don't feel safe trying to wait this out."

"They've left us alone so far?" Terre asked absently.

"Nobody lives in this neighborhood yet," she replied. "Wouldn't be a high priority target."

Terre shook his head. A jet flew past, and he watched a light emanate from it toward the mass of drones still in the sky.

There was hardly a flash, but the lights of the drones all winked out simultaneously as a blue pulse emanated from the projectile hurled at them and the jet flared, racing off into the distance. The three orbs hovering above the city remained stationary, unmoved by whatever force had grounded the smaller drones.

"Standard EMP?" Terre asked.

"The Air Force has been doing their best to ground the micros. Gotta say, they've been doing a damn good job."

"Still no activity from the Onyx?"

"Your boy must be hanging on for the big finale," Hailey said. "But I'm surprised the President hasn't given the order to blast them out of the sky."

"That call will render trillions of dollars worth of tech useless," Terre offered, doing up a missed button on his shirt. "NextGen3 tech is in the prototype phase. Any lost units would have a devastating economic effect on our military capability. And the kind of EMP needed to put an end to this siege couldn't be limited to just the bots. Would you want to be the President who made the call to send Las Vegas back into the Stone Age for the next couple centuries?"

Only then did he realize the tough decisions the higher uppers would face right at that moment. Sitting in their boxed offices, going over reports sent in from across the country. And who knew how many other cities were being affected? They were essentially completely cut off from the rest of the nation. There was potentially only one person Terre could talk to who might know what in the world was truly happening.

They had to find K before things escalated even further.

Terre lifted a hand to his forehead, rubbing it against the smoothness of his skin. He wondered briefly if the nanos in his bloodstream would ever allow the effects of time to reach his appearance, but he supposed he'd have to live long enough to find out before that would matter.

"You geeks are *way* too overprotective when it comes to your toys," Hailey answered. "But I guess that's what happens when you let short-sighted people play with them. If I were President, I'd have realized that AI has more potential to aid humanity beyond being utilities of war."

Terre adjusted his flannel shirt so that he could move his arms without tearing the sleeves. "What are you really after,

Hailey? Something's not adding up. You're sent on this mission to track me down; to follow me and make sure I can talk some sense into Klein. Yet you're a trans-humanist? How does that add up?"

"Human evolution and military bullshit are two very different things."

"You work for the Agency," Terre said, weighing the weight of her words. "How did that happen? Surely their objectives defy your ambitions. They've sent you on a mission to stop all this."

"I'm on a mission to stop *Klein*," Hailey replied. "Humanity isn't smart enough to handle what's coming."

Terre raised an eyebrow. "Not quite the future you had in mind?"

"This country has always picked itself up and been made strong through adversity. Sometimes we don't get the events we expect, but we're made tougher for them anyhow."

"Well, I haven't given up yet." There had to be a way to stop the assault before it got to the point of Armageddon. Hailey might be ready to take K out no questions asked, but Terre knew that whatever K was up to, it was likely a plan to finally put this entire robot bullshit to rest. He had to hold on to that hope.

"We should head out," he said.

"Wake the others and we'll be on our way. I'm going to load the SUV." Hailey uncrossed her arms, picked up an armful of supplies, and left.

Terre shook his head as he watched the light cresting over the desert surrounding the subdivision they found themselves in. The Strip, now miles away, was eerily quiet. He knew it was an illusion. Thousands would be now waking within the stadiums, the decimated hotel towers, and artificial landscapes contained in a constructed amusement park for adults—now a prison of terror.

A line of headlights on a nearby freeway heading into the

city caught Terre's eye. He could vaguely make out the square bulky shapes of what he could only assume were military vehicles.

They're going to try and evacuate the city.

There were so many city residents who would need to be escorted elsewhere. How many people must be located nearby? A million? Would it be feasible to evacuate so many people without the technology they had all become so dependent on? How many vehicles would Homeland Security be able to round up without AI assistance?

Terre didn't know how, but so much of the future of the city—of the *country*—seemed to depend on what he could discover within the next few hours.

"I thought you were waking them?" Hailey barked as she re-entered the room.

Terre shook himself out of his thoughts. "Sorry," he said. "I guess I'm still waking up myself."

He moved to rouse the women as Hailey huffed and grabbed another armful of supplies.

Chapter Fourteen

Terre

It struck Terre as odd that he was even slightly disturbed by Hailey abandoning the bodies of Harold and Frank out in the desert. As they started out on the second day of their journey, Annika and Hailey filled him in on the grisly details of what had happened after he'd passed out.

The terrorists had chocked the Ford pickup full of essential items. Blankets and flannel shirts were only the beginning; the vehicle also contained canned food, water, and toiletries. There were enough supplies to have lasted the pair of lowlifes at least a month, if not more. Hailey, Annika, and Becky had painstakingly taken as many of the items as they could fit in the back of their SUV.

"Just in case," Hailey said.

"In case of what?" Terre asked.

Hailey didn't answer. Instead, she pursed her lips and looked away.

"You don't think the rest of their group, this Robot Resistance, will come looking for them?" Terre asked.

Hailey simply shrugged. The morning sun revealed the bags under her eyes. The water had been turned off along with the power, so none of them were looking as fresh as they would have liked without a welcome shower. They both appeared tired and worn after restless nights. Terre caught a glimpse of himself in the side-view mirror and cringed. He was apparently no exception.

"That depends on how well they were liked." Hailey offered a sly grin. "So, I'd guess probably not. Besides, there's a regimented order to these groups: if something goes wrong, the rest of the group continues with the plan to ensure they reach their destination. They'll have arranged a rendezvous point to ensure any survivors will eventually catch up. If what Annika says proves true, and the Resistance we're planning on hiding out in the mountains to the west, the rest of the group would assume that if Harold and Frank don't show up, they're dead."

Terre nodded. "I just don't want a horde of terrorists on our tail while we're headed into a snake pit of bots."

"They have bigger things to worry about than us. They didn't even bother to wait around for the pair to catch up with them. I stand by what I said; they either weren't well liked, or their caravan was instructed to carry on, no matter what."

Hailey's rationale still didn't sit well with Terre, but there was nothing to be done about it now. They were well on their way, and if they were being followed, he supposed they would have most likely been assaulted during their stay at the house, not the next day on the road.

They had avoided the freeway and stuck to the back roads as much as possible. Abandoned vehicles still jammed the roadways, and they couldn't afford to crawl along at the pace that avoiding them required.

"Besides, we should be focusing on dodging any other bots that might be marching on the city," Hailey said. "We don't want to be forced into a fight or having to hide."

"How many do you think are out there?" Annika asked

from the back seat. "There had to have been nearly a hundred earlier."

"You don't want to know," Terre answered, surveying the mountainous terrain ahead of them. The last image he had seen after he and Kristopher had uploaded The Guardian Program in San Francisco still haunted him: hundreds of eyes coming to life in the final moments before the power was cut. Sentinel units had been displayed, row upon row, in warehouses spread throughout the country. And Terre knew the ones in storage were only a fraction of what the military had developed, placed on standby in case of emergency situations.

Somehow, nobody in the administration had had the foresight to plan for what happened if the bots themselves were causing the emergency.

"Human ingenuity knows no bounds," he said when Annika offered him a puzzled look. "Rarely do we ask ourselves if we're too smart for our own good. We've developed tech capable of outpacing our ability to keep up with it, and it looks like nobody ever stopped to ask if it was a good idea."

"I still don't understand why the bots are attacking civilians?" Becky jumped in. "Aren't they meant to be soldiers? Wouldn't their creators have programmed them with some sort of safeguards?"

"You would have thought so," Terre scoffed. "But obviously their programming has been compromised." *Because of my actions.* "All I know is, whatever glitch is causing these things to attack us, it's also overriding their ability to decipher friend from foe. We're all designated targets within their operating systems now."

Becky scrunched her face, as though trying to parse the information. "Didn't you say you were the one who stopped them in San Fran?" She let the end of her question hang, as though she couldn't quite believe the man who sat before her was capable of derailing an army of death machines.

"*Kristopher* was, mostly," Terre replied. "I just did my best to keep him alive."

And killed the upload before it was complete.

"But it didn't work," she said decisively. "That's why everyone's after him." Becky nodded as though satisfied by her own answer, and to Terre's relief, she let the matter drop, resigning herself to look out the window once again.

"Something's off," Hailey said suddenly, scratching her temple with her chipped pink nails.

"What do you mean?" Terre asked.

"We're just outside Boulder City, but we haven't seen any vehicles for the last five miles."

"These back roads are always less busy. Maybe we just got lucky."

Hailey scoffed. "*Lucky*? Yeah, right. Anyway, the town's just ahead. Prepare yourselves, people. We don't know what we're going to find."

Terre didn't know how much more prepared he could be. If what had happened in Vegas was any indication of how things were elsewhere, there wasn't anything he could do except watch for signs of an ambush.

Sunlight reflected on the haze of the desert as they approached. Wind kicked up sand, masking the hillside before them, producing an eerie calm that had Terre on the edge of his seat.

"Do you smell that?" Hailey asked suddenly, lifting her nose to the air.

Terre mimicked her, trying to get a whiff of whatever it was the woman smelled. Mostly, all he got was the slightly sweet lingering of dust covering the SUV. Terre was used to a more tropical climate, and the arid Nevada environment was parching his senses. The desert air grated against his skin and his eyes had felt like sandpaper for the past few days, and the sensation was even more pronounced out in the open landscape.

"I can't smell a damn thing," he answered. "What are you picking up?"

Hailey furrowed her brow, as though trying to decide. "Burning."

"Maybe someone lit a fire to cook up some breakfast," he suggested. "If the power's out here as well, perhaps someone just needed to prepare a meal. Or maybe its the remnants of an overnight campfire?"

"No, it's not that." Hailey shook her head. "I don't know. Maybe I'm just imagining it."

"You're not." Annika was practically standing in the back seat, one hand up to block the sun from her eyes and the other pointing out the side of the SUV toward Boulder City. Black plumes billowed above the valley.

"Buckle up," Hailey said stoically. "Looks like we're headed right into the thick of it."

Chapter Fifteen

Terre

It had been Terre's freshman year at college when he'd decided to pursue what he had believed to be the adventure of a lifetime.

He couldn't imagine a better way to spend the summer than working at the Hoover Dam. He knew it was a nerdy obsession, but the Hoover Dam was not only a marvel of architecture, ingenuity, and an emblem of the American spirit, it was also being upgraded to full automation. The construction itself proved humanity still had dominion over the land, and that with enough engineering, intellect, and technology, humanity could accomplish just about anything.

Built to control the Boulder River in the 1930s to prevent flooding, provide a means for farmers to irrigate the land, and produce power for the southwestern part of the country, the site itself was a marvel. The sheer audacity of now automating such an integral part of American infrastructure had fascinated Terre, and to see it firsthand was an opportunity he couldn't turn down.

So, in his mind, it had made sense to leave the confines of MIT to pursue the rugged outback of Nevada for a season.

Terre had found a room to rent in the basement of Ms.

Walters's home, a kind-hearted, middle-aged woman who had just lost her son deployed overseas and wanted a few things fixed around the house in exchange for room and board. Terre had never been handy, but with a little help from a few friends and instructional videos he'd found online, he'd managed to get Ms. Walters's lawnmower, clothes dryer, and toilet all up and running again.

It had been a memorable summer; the kind you can only have when you're nineteen, consumed by reckless abandon. The city was a boon for retirees and summer students. Otherwise, its residents had mostly been those who worked at the Dam.

Terre would have smiled at the memory if he could. Instead, his jaw hung open, his gut feeling as though someone had knocked the wind right out of him.

As they approached the city, the smoke Hailey had faintly smelled fifteen minutes prior lay thick, threatening to choke out their small party.

The SUV rolled through the decimated city. Gas stations, coffee shops, fast-food restaurants—all of it was gone. Shattered glass, collapsed rooftops, and torn down signage lay strewn in fragments across the cratered highway. Terre didn't need to ask what had caused the damage. Blaster marks scarred the remnants of the once bustling community.

"Where are all the people?" Annika asked, her eyes watering from the smoke.

Terre had also noticed the absence of residents himself. He was immensely grateful the death and carnage were hidden from sight, but it highlighted the unnatural circumstances of the attack. "Either they've escaped or they're dead."

"Let's hope they saw the attack coming and made a run for it," Annika offered.

It was a nice sentiment, but Terre had his doubts. An

entire city with the foresight to pack up and leave? It seemed unlikely.

Yet, as he looked around, he saw no signs of death. No bodies; no blood; nothing that showed anyone had remained in the city to fight back. There was not a single sign of the body count he'd expect to accompany the amount of the destruction that lay before them. He silently prayed that the townspeople of Boulder City had some place safe to go.

"The vehicles here haven't been used," Hailey commented. "It's as if they've been put away neatly, instead of stopped haphazardly on the main road."

Terre tried to survey the parking lots and streets as best he could through the smoke. Hailey was right; the automated vehicles here weren't the obstacles they had been in Vegas. Instead, it was as if they were waiting patiently for their owners to return.

A wave of despair washed over Terre, and he gripped the doorframe beside him in the hope of keeping his mood stable. Even if the people here had escaped with their lives, what else did they have? Their belongings, their homes, maybe even their families, were all gone. The Sentinels had pounded through Boulder and imposed that these people would never again live a normal life.

Terre wondered how many citizens had lost their jobs, either at the Dam or elsewhere, long ago? How many had already barely been hanging on? Where could they possibly go to that would provide them with more hope than they had here?

Will there be anywhere for any of us to go?

A city now smoldered in the aftermath of human innovation. A city that could have been any of thousands across the country. Why here? Why Boulder City? What did the bots stand to gain by bringing the city to its knees? Perhaps there were thousands more like it. Terre had no way of knowing. His phone had died overnight, so not even Fredricks could now give him an answer.

His resolve to find K strengthened. Terre had no idea what to expect when he found the man, but, damn it, he wouldn't accept that K had any role in provoking the destruction of Boulder City, no more than he believed the man could have had a hand in the Sentinels' descent on Vegas. It didn't matter what Hailey believed, or even Fredricks; the man Terre had spent those weeks with in San Francisco was not capable of advocating such destruction, no matter how broken the fight against the bots had left him.

"Do you hear that?" Hailey asked, craning her neck downtown.

"What is it?" Terre tried to follow her gaze. In the distance, a plume of dust rose, darkening the still thick smoke rising from the nearby buildings.

"A vehicle," Hailey said, nodding at the same plume that had caught Terre's eye.

Whoever was driving had no qualms about moving quickly through the haze. Terre noticed Hailey had picked up their own pace as well, whether subconsciously or intentionally, to get past whoever was coming toward them at breakneck speed.

"Are we expecting company?" Annika's grip was tight around the headrest in front of her, pulling herself closer to the front seat so she could be part of their conversation.

"Not from anybody we want to meet," Hailey replied.

"You don't know that," Terre said. "Maybe they're looking for survivors?"

"Nobody looking for survivors travels the back roads that fast."

Terre's hand reached for his blaster as three dark-colored trucks turned onto their street and continued toward them.

"We can't outrun them in this," Terre said, nodding to the

blanket of smog that enveloped them. "It won't matter what their intentions are if we kill ourselves in the process."

Hailey cursed as she pulled the steering wheel to the side, swerving the SUV about-face in a single, smooth motion, tires screeching as their momentum shifted and brought them to a halt.

"No blasters," Hailey said, and she turned to eye Annika in the backseat. "And no guns, either. Not until we know their intentions."

Terre raised an eyebrow, keeping his hand firmly on his CD-115.

The three trucks stopped in the middle of the street, their frames sitting side by side, taking up most of the lane space. Hailey wouldn't be driving through their blockade without some fancy maneuvering. Though Terre was certain the woman could pull it off, she showed no sign of taking the chance. Where Hailey had stopped had left a few driveways open between their vehicle and the ones that had just arrived. If they had a bit of a lead and some luck, he was sure she'd be able to steer them past any threat if she needed to.

If they weren't being shot at.

As truck doors swung open down the road, Terre caught his breath.

A getaway might be a good plan.

A man and a woman stepped out of the center vehicle. The first thing Terre noticed was, they were armed. *Heavily* armed. Terre didn't know much about weaponry, but he knew automatic rifles when he saw them. He held his breath. Whoever these people were, they weren't messing around. The cold metal of his blaster rested beneath his palm, but he knew his aim was awful, and he hazarded a guess that even if these newcomers were equally bad shots, they'd fire enough rounds to make up for it.

"Don't make any sudden moves," Hailey cautioned.

Terre bit his lip to hold back another of his signature smart-ass comments.

Both individuals wore sunglasses and combat boots and were decked from head-to-toe as if they were ready for war.

Better prepared than the rest of us, Terre thought snidely.

Though, on second glance, Terre realized that perhaps the pair weren't *quite* as ready as they were making themselves out to be.

'Better equipped' might have been a better way of putting it. Behind the aviator glasses, the man was skinny and soft, and his arms didn't quite fill the tactical vest he had on, its black Teflon noticeably contrasting with his sandy skin. The man's face betrayed his youth—he couldn't have been much older than twenty-two—and Terre would lay all his chips down on him having spent more time in front of a screen than behind a weapon.

The youth's confidence was fresh. He stood a little too straight, as though only recently aware that he possessed any sort of power.

Similarly, the woman was, at first, intimidating, but on closer inspection, she appeared unnatural in the tactical get-up. Her vest fit more snugly than her companion's, but it wasn't due to muscle. Her blonde hair was shoulder length and clean. Either she had been spending most of her time since the attack indoors, or she had access to fresh water and accessories. There was a faint tremble in her stance that Terre probably would have missed if he hadn't spent the last two years around military men and women, and he had seen enough weapons drills and training to know she was uncomfortable with the bulk of the M4 Carbine she held.

"Please get out of the vehicle," the man ordered. "And keep your hands where we can see them."

Terre exchanged a look with Hailey, who gave him a curt nod, before he slowly opened the SUV door and raised his hands high to show he didn't intend to reach for the weapon that hung from his hip. Hailey did the same.

"You shouldn't be here," the woman remarked. "It'd be best if you turned around and headed back to wherever you came from." Her voice was assured; confident and even. Her accent was light but reminded Terre of the West Coast. She held her weapon in front of her without aiming, which slightly calmed Terre's nerves, though he'd have probably felt better if he believed she knew what she was doing with it. Or even better, if she wasn't holding a weapon at all.

The man beside her shifted his weight uncomfortably, as though the mass of the gear he was equipped with was too much for him to hold.

"We're not looking for trouble," Hailey said, her open palms held up. "We just need to pass through here, to the Dam. We're looking for someone."

"The Dam's closed, ma'am," the woman replied. "Nobody is allowed past here. For your own protection."

Hailey rolled her eyes and took a step forward. "Protection from who?" she scoffed. "You?"

It was quick, but Terre caught the uncertain glance that passed between the two newcomers.

"Who are you?" he interjected before they could reply. "What gives you any right to turn us away?"

"This is *our* city," the young man said, shaking off any hesitation and moving back toward bravado. "There's nobody left here. And we're gonna keep it that way."

Terre tried to hold back a laugh. The tough guy was just a kid; someone who had managed to survive the attack on the city by hiding in his parents' basement. The gear he sported was probably his father's.

Terre shook his head and took a step forward. "That's not how this is going to go."

He didn't make any threatening moves. Despite the brave face, the kid was scared; that much was obvious. Terre didn't want to risk prompting a rash move from someone who was afraid for their own safety. Terre had no doubt the two armed citizens might lift their weapons if they felt their hold on the situation was slipping.

"We're not going to hurt you, and we're not looking to take anything. We just want to pass through."

"*That's* what we're telling you." The waves in the woman's hair bounced as she swung her M4 Carbine up to her shoulder. "There's no stayin', and there's no passing through." Her nervousness had disappeared, the waiver in her grip gone and her feet firmly planted.

"I'd think carefully about your next move," Hailey warned, her own CD-115 now out of its holster but still held against the leg of her pants. The blaster was ready if she had to use it, but she was making an effort to telegraph she didn't want to.

"Funny," the blonde said. "I was about to tell you the same thing."

Movement from behind the pair caught Terre's eye, and he whipped his blaster up in reflex.

"Friends," a voice called out from behind the first pickup. The doors to both vehicles beyond had opened without Terre even realizing.

His heart raced. They had been tricked.

They were about to be ambushed.

His pulse drummed in his ears as Terre belatedly scanned his surroundings. Two men stood on the right-hand side of the road, pistols drawn. A woman stood on their left, mimicking them.

Terre lifted his hands, his blaster going slack against his palm. There'd be no winning whatever fight these folks were bringing to the table.

"Let's not be hasty!" the voice of a sixth person boomed.

Terre couldn't make out the man who stood behind the

vehicle door, his features just out of his line of vision, but the voice sounded all too familiar.

Terre craned his head as much as he dared, enough to catch a glimpse of a shaggy mop of black hair atop a pasty white face.

"You have *got* to be shitting me!"

Chapter Sixteen

Annika

Annika couldn't hear a word over the thumping of her own heart and Becky's whimpering.

What she perceived were the tightened spines, deadpan glares, and raised brows as Terre and Hailey spotted the men and women who had crept up toward them from the second and third trucks. Annika had seen them approaching, and she'd considered racing out to warn them of the potential danger, but she'd thought better of it. Terre and Hailey were far more perceptive than her, so if she had spotted a potential ambush, they would surely be aware of it themselves. There was no need to escalate the situation.

But the way Terre had reacted to their arrival was all Annika needed to know for her to realize she had been mistaken. The occupants of the first truck had engaged the agents in conversation; a planned deception. Their big talk was nothing more than a ruse to ensure no brash moves could be made, or their small party decided to escape.

Annika had watched the blonde carefully. The woman's movements were calculated, as though she was pretending to be incompetent, duping Terre with her charade. She was doing a damn good job of it, too. Though Annika couldn't hear the words the woman spoke, she caught the tone. Feigned nerves disguised an air of confidence, played up as though the opposite were true.

If it wasn't for the appearance of the shaggy-haired man who came up from the rear of the ambush, Annika would have thought their worst fears were about to become reality. It would have been all too easy for the group to take out Terre and Hailey before she'd be able to get more than a shot or two off to defend them, which meant she and Becky would be left to their own fates. Annika felt the cold steel of the gun she had swiped from Harold with her palm. She had it drawn, but she wasn't in any way close to being ready to fire. Using the weapon would possibly buy them a minute or two, but Annika eyed the automatic weapons the vigilantes held and knew her imagined victory would be short-lived.

Everything had changed as soon as the shaggy-haired man had stepped out from behind the trucks. Annika wasn't sure why he had held back until then, but at the sound of his voice, the tension among the rest dissipated. Including Terre.

Hailey, on the other hand, appeared to be more stressed. Her lips curled back in a snarl.

"Do you mind telling me why you have a gang of nerds pointing their guns at us?" Terre called out, loud enough for Annika to hear.

The man let out a quick burst of laughter and held up a gloved hand. The black glove was fingerless, stylish, and it perfectly complemented the man's mop of black hair and long trench coat. Annika was wearing jeans and an appropriated T-shirt she had scrounged from the duffle bag containing Harold and Frank's belongings, and even in the lightweight attire, sweat glistened on her forehead and arms. Yet the man before them didn't look to be fazed by the heat, despite being so heavily clothed.

"It's all right, folks." The man lifted his hands, a big, toothy grin taking over his face. "Lower your weapons."

The posture of the armed men and women visibly relaxed as they put their weapons away and looked at each other, confused.

Annika figured it was as good a moment as any to exit the vehicle, so she prodded Becky, who nodded, receiving the unspoken intent.

They had only been driving for an hour, but it felt as though Annika had been in the car for days, her muscles stiff and her joints creaking. She assumed most of the strain was from the exertions of the day before. Running through the streets of Vegas now felt like a lifetime ago; a lifetime where things made sense. Now, she stood in the middle of the highway, the structures all around her destroyed by robotic soldiers and the stench of gasoline permeating the air, with a gang of ruffians holding them at gunpoint. And, somehow, the man who had brought her here knew the ringleader. A wave of panic crept over Annika. What if this was all a setup? What if Terre had brought her here for the purpose of delivering them to this place? Perhaps she wouldn't have been any worse off with the Robot Resistance, after all.

Her head spun, but the weight of a friendly hand and a questioning look from Becky snapped her back to reality.

Becky, sensing Annika's questions and her panic, nodded to Hailey. The woman had lowered her weapon, but she hadn't put it away yet. She was suspicious of the raiders as much as anyone, yet she seemed more annoyed than worried, which at least gave Annika temporary reassurance. It had been Hailey's idea to drive them out this way. She had been at the wheel; it would have been a lot harder to pull Hailey into a trap, if that was what Terre had been planning.

"I'd like to say it's good to see you, K," Terre continued. "What the hell are you doing here?"

K? This was the man Terre was looking for? The roboticist?

"You know why I'm here, Terre. Fredricks drilled into me

that it was up to *me* to save the world." K's face split with a grin. "I guess I had a hard time letting that go."

Terre paused, a hand lifting to scratch the side of his head. Annika could see the questions churning in his mind, just as they were in her own.

Hailey's hand flexed around her weapon.

Annika looked from her to Terre, who hadn't noticed that the other agent was still on edge.

"What happened here?" Terre asked. "Where is everybody?"

"Most of them left before the attack. But they're leading the kids out into the desert." A wild look crossed K's green eyes. His gaze flicked from Terre to Hailey to the other gunmen that stood around them, seemingly without focus. "The Sentinels slaughtered half the city before we helped the rest to escape. A classic vehicle collector in the city's outskirts allowed us to commandeer these vehicles. We got as many out as we could. The survivors have set up camp in the mountains, but the kids … We haven't got the kids back."

"Easy, buddy." Terre lifted a hand. "You're not making sense. *Who* is leading the kids into the desert?"

Annika didn't need to hear to the response to know the answer.

"The bots." Kristopher gave Terre a dumbfounded look, as though he didn't understand how Terre wasn't putting the pieces together faster.

"Where did they go?" Annika puffed her chest and held her head high. She wasn't about to let her anxiety show to the rebels. She had never seen the types of guns they carried before, and despite knowing Terre knew this man, her heart hadn't stopped pounding since they arrived, but she had to know where Ember had taken Cheyenne. She had to know if her sister was okay, and she had put off the search for too long already. It was time for answers.

Kristopher started, as though he had forgotten there was

anyone else standing around besides Terre and himself. He took a deep breath, his eyes continuing to dart between their small group before his eyes landed back on Terre. "You've made some new friends."

"Answer the question," Terre said, his arms crossing over his chest.

Annika couldn't help but feel a smidge of satisfaction at Terre's assurance.

Kristopher raised a brow. "The bots rounded up the kids from here and led them to a facility they've been building near the Hoover Dam. Kids from elsewhere, too, from what we've learned. Then Sentinels came through; tried to kill the rest. Destroyed the town in the process."

"We don't have time for this," Hailey butted in, taking a step forward and challenging Kristopher directly. "What are you doing to the bots? Why have they been reactivated?"

The rebels lifted their guns again, all pointed in her direction. Her hands went up reflexively, but she didn't back down.

Kristopher appeared annoyed, running both hands through his mop of hair, his mouth hanging open in agitation.

"*Ugh*. Who's this?" he said, addressing Terre once again. "Fredricks sent you, didn't he? Come to check up on what we're doing out here? To see why we're scaring people away from their glorious bots?"

"K, calm down," Terre said reassuringly. "You're not making sense."

"Aren't I?" K seethed. "I've spent the last few weeks trying to stop them; trying to figure out how to make this all go away. Instead, I had to fight alongside the residents of this city. This godforsaken city, whose people wouldn't believe they needed to move until a hoard of robot soldiers were descending upon them, blowing holes through their shops and homes. And what help did our esteemed government give to protect the innocent here? *Nothing.* Instead, it seems, they're more concerned with what *I'm* doing. Damn it, Terre! Didn't you stop to think about what's happening for two minutes?"

Kristopher nodded to the gunmen closest to Hailey. The two of them returned the gesture and moved to disarm her.

"I've been doing nothing *but* trying to put the pieces together since Fredricks made the call," Terre responded. "I was enjoying a nice glass of scotch in Las Vegas before all of this started. Believe me, I'd rather be sitting at the bar sharing my woes with the robot bartender than trying to make sense of your mad ramblings. What's really going on, K?"

Annika wasn't sure what to think. The robotics expert seemed completely insane, and she doubted he was going to be of any further help in finding Cheyenne. She was losing time. Up to now, sticking with Terre and Hailey had been the best option, but now she found herself caught up in whatever beef they had with the madman delaying them. Maybe it was time for them all to part ways.

"I don't care what you're doing here," she said, not giving Kristopher the chance to respond and surprising herself with the steadiness of her own voice. "I don't care who you are, or what Terre or Hailey want from you. I just came to find my sister. I've got no fight with you."

"And we've got more important objectives than a kid and her wayward bot." Hailey didn't look at Annika as she dismissed her concerns in front of everyone else. "We need answers about what's happening, Klein. If you're behind the AI malfunctions and power outages, now's the time to come clean."

Kristopher threw back his head in laughter, but Annika barely heard it. Hailey had bulldozed right over her attempt to reason with him.

Terre's focus was completely on Kristopher.

"Come on." Becky ripped Annika from her spinning thoughts. "They've got their own stuff to deal with. This isn't helping Cheyenne."

Annika could have kissed her friend at that moment; the one loyal friend she had who knew what she needed to hear.

She smiled but then looked at the gunmen, and her good mood soured. Annika sighed. If this man decided he wanted them to be a part of whatever game he was playing with Terre, she wasn't sure they'd be able to fight their way out; not without Terre and Hailey giving them covering fire, at least. And deep down, Annika knew she wouldn't be able to rely on Terre's help any longer. But what if she failed? What if she found herself in another bind she couldn't get out of? Who would come rescue her then?

She had already tried to go it alone twice in the past twenty-four hours and had failed miserably.

Strangely, the programmer turned to her and said indifferently, "You're right, lady. I don't have any fight with you. If you want to take off, be my guest."

His unexpected words left Annika speechless. She'd figured he would be resistant to letting any of them leave, but as she started to step backward, none of the group's guns began tracking her. Becky gave her a smirk, but her eyes reflected Annika's apprehension about the bold move before following.

Terre turned to Annika, his eyes boring into her. "You sure you want to do this?"

Her eyes met his. "Thank you so much for all you've done for us, but this isn't our fight."

"Take a look around, Annika—it's *everyone's* fight."

The city before them was aflame.

Annika swallowed the lump that formed in her throat. "I'm sorry, Terre. I have to."

Strangely, Terre smiled. "I get it. Good luck."

Annika reached for Becky's arm to direct her, nodded to

Hailey, and began to walk away. She'd barely gotten twenty yards before she heard the programmer's raised voice following her.

"If your sister was taken by the bots," Kristopher called out, "you won't get her back."

Chapter Seventeen

Annika

Annika froze mid-step. In the distance, glass crashed as fire dislodged it from its pane, but she didn't react. Becky stopped short just behind her, and the ever-supportive friend put a warm hand on her shoulder. Grime from the day's journey clung to Annika's skin beneath Becky's grip on her shirt.

For a moment, she deliberated whether she should turn and face the accusation head on or ignore it, to simply continue into the wilderness.

Annika's gut told her to listen to the man, or at least to question his reasoning. Her heart was already a mile ahead of her, running into the unknown in search of the only person who had mattered to her for the past seven years. Both parts of her agreed that giving up on her sister wasn't an answer.

But in that moment of pause, her gut and her head began talking to each other, reminding Annika of the last time she had run headstrong into the desert and where it had gotten her. One look at the pillaged town around her was all it took to realize that the Robot Resistance wouldn't be the only ones crazed or desperate enough to do something brash to two unprepared women on the run. Nor would they be the worst of the threats that lay ahead.

She needed to find Cheyenne, but something about the abnormal tone Klein's last words to her had conveyed threw her off her game. She was out of her depth, and though she didn't want to be caught up in anything which kept her off course from reuniting with her sister, Annika began to realize that no matter her level of determination, no matter the desperation she felt, and no matter the amount of will she had in seeking her out, she needed help to do that.

And despite Becky's support and willingness to follow Annika to Hades if need be, Annika's friend was just as ill-prepared for what was out there as she was.

But nobody was going to stop her from trying.

Annika shuffled her feet and turned to look into the green eyes of the shaggy-haired man. "I will find my sister. No bot is going to stop me."

The wind picked up, blowing sand and smoke through their group. Kristopher Klein stood immobile, returning Annika's stare with steadfast will and determination. Out of the corner of her eye, Annika could see Terre, his own gaze locked on Kristopher. Hailey was staring at Annika, making no effort to hide her annoyance at being disrupted in progressing with her mission.

Annika ignored the other woman's glare, keeping her eyes glued to the man before her until her eyes watered from the dry desert air and were stinging from the smoke.

"What do you know about this facility you mentioned, K?" Terre broke the silence and the concentration of the other man. "Sounds like there's every chance Annika's sister's there."

A wry smile crossed Kristopher's face, as if the whole situation were a joke. Breaking his gaze from Annika, he turned his attention back to Terre.

"Always a sucker for a kid in distress, aren't you, Terre?

Yes, if the bots took your sister, I can get you there, but you aren't going to like it."

"There's nothing about the last twenty-four hours I've liked," Annika replied. "But I won't abandon her."

Kristopher turned his wry smile back to Annika. His eyes betrayed his true feelings, though. There was fear in those eyes. Fear and regret.

"I don't think this is a laughing matter, Klein," Hailey said, her hand still on her weapon.

Annika was beginning to think the woman wouldn't hesitate to use it, regardless of the outcome for the rest of them.

"Indeed," Kristopher replied. His gaze didn't leave Annika, though.

There was a pain beneath his smile—an anguish Kristopher was attempting to mask. Or maybe it was deflection of pain—or guilt, perhaps. Annika had seen enough tired souls who had given up their farmland in defeat; enough folks who had toiled endlessly to keep their livelihood before finally giving up after admitting they were holding on in vain to a past that would never exist again. For a while, they put on a brave face, but it wasn't long after that a person fell apart completely.

"I'll take you to the place where the bots are probably holding your sister." Kristopher nodded, his eyes dropping slightly in what could have been either sadness or regret. They hardened again before turning to Hailey for the first time. "And I'll show you what we've been struggling against. Not that I imagine you'll care—or that it'll matter for much longer."

"And who are these guys?" Terre waved a hand at the armed men and women who had aligned themselves with the robotics specialist.

"Classmates, coworkers," Kristopher answered. "Some of the best programmers in our field."

Terre smirked. "Nerds with guns."

"Maybe not such a bad idea after all." Kristopher grinned, but it still didn't reach his eyes.

Something passed between the two men, though Annika couldn't tell what it was. A connection, or an inside joke.

"Ride with me," Kristopher continued. "We'll talk on the way. Bring the woman looking for her sister. Her friend and the agent can follow us."

Terre beckoned for Annika to join them. She gave Becky a skeptical glance.

"I'll be okay," Becky assured her. "Let's at least see where Cheyenne's at. I'll be right behind you."

Something didn't seem right. Annika didn't like the fact that she was being separated from her friend. Kristopher wasn't telling them much about what was happening, or what his role was in all of this. At least the man believed he was saving the world. That was a start, she guessed.

Annika shared a brief look with Hailey, who, surprisingly, seemed to share some of her reservations.

Hailey shook it off, her determination strengthening once again. "Oh, hell no! I didn't drag this guy's ass all the way out here for you two to go riding off into the sunset like Bonnie and Clyde. Or for you to put a bullet in his head and take off into the desert."

Kristopher glanced back with a smirk. "If I were going to shoot anyone here, it certainly wouldn't be Terre."

"Look around, Hailey." Terre stepped in. "If they wanted us dead, they'd have opened fire by now! And where do you think we're going to run to? You easily tracked me down before, and I'm guessing you'd do it again. I was sent here to talk to K. Let me talk to him."

Kristopher raised an eyebrow but didn't respond.

Hailey gritted her teeth, but she let the matter lie. "Come on then, Becky." The statement was more of a sneer. "Let's let the nerds talk."

Annika wasn't sure who she trusted less at this point: Terre, Kristopher, or Hailey. Terre, at least, had saved her life more than once, but Annika had to admit she knew little about Hailey's or the programmer's motives. There was undoubtedly something off about Kristopher. His wild appearance didn't help matters, but there was a certain rugged attractiveness to the sprawling black hair and unshaven face. But it was his eyes that worried Annika; she saw a waywardness within them that didn't sit quite right with her.

Then there was Hailey. Something had changed in the woman since finding Kristopher. From the conversations she'd overheard, Klein was Hailey's primary mission objective, so Annika presumed her behavior was a by-product of being faced with its completion. After seeing the way Hailey had held off a handful of Sentinel bots by herself, Annika didn't believe for a second a few computer scientists intimidated the woman.

No, it was almost as if the woman saw a window of opportunity closing. Annika had overheard Hailey talking about taking Kristopher out if Terre's talks with him didn't prove fruitful. But surely the woman was willing to at least allow Terre to talk to the man; to determine his purpose before she acted. Wasn't she?

Annika had to admit, the pieces hadn't exactly been stacking up to reveal Kristopher's innocence. The destroyed town, the group of vigilante nerds—and their arrival was oddly convenient.

The best in their field.

If there was ever a group able to hack into the necessary systems, it was this one.

Annika shook off the thoughts. None of that mattered. There was nothing she could do to change the tidal wave of events that were transpiring. Terre and Hailey had problems rooted in national secrets Annika had no knowledge of, nor did she care to. Only along for the ride, she was a Canadian with no interest in American national security policy, related to bots or otherwise. If it wasn't for sheer desperation in finding Cheyenne, she wouldn't be in the middle of the godforsaken desert with a madman and two CIA agents with seemingly opposing agendas.

Hailey and Becky had already climbed into the SUV. Terre was staring at Annika, waiting for her response.

"You coming or not?" he asked.

Klein's knowledge of the bots' facility was the only lead Annika had for where Cheyenne might be, and on that basis alone, it was worth taking the chance. Besides, Terre hadn't let her down so far. But, for one last time, she still weighed if it was worth climbing into a vehicle with a potentially unstable robotics analyst in order to find her sister.

She knew the answer.

At least this way, Terre wouldn't have to come running to her rescue once again.

Chapter Eighteen

Terre

"How well do you know her?" Kristopher asked as he closed the door to the truck, the weight of the metal frame clunking as it ground against the doorframe.

"Who?" Terre replied. "Annika? I just met her yesterday, but she's as nice as the Canadian stereotype. A little headstrong. Tends to get herself into rough situations." He glanced back at Annika in the back seat and thought he saw her blush. "But she's determined, and she's not afraid to kill a man to protect someone she cares about."

Annika's mouth hung open at the last bit, but K cut in before she could say anything.

"Not *her*, dumbass!" K snapped, before glancing back at Annika in the rearview mirror. "No offense. It's nice to meet you."

Annika gave a half-hearted, wary smile and a nod. "Likewise," she said.

Terre couldn't help but grin.

"Canadian? I've got an aunt that lives near Vancouver. Nice place except…"

"Could we get to the point?" Terre interrupted.

K returned to glaring at Terre. "The other woman," he

said. "The one with the CD-115. How well do you know her?"

K yanked the truck into gear and cranked the steering wheel, turning the truck around a hundred and eighty degrees and onto the highway.

"Her name's Hailey. I met her at the bar last night. She's involved with the Agency somehow, though she hasn't told me much." Terre didn't think it'd be wise to tell the man sitting next to him that she'd also admitted she'd kill him if Terre couldn't sort things out.

"She's not who she says she is," K replied pointedly. "I don't trust her."

"What do you mean? How do you know her?"

"I don't, but she doesn't seem too interested in finding out what's going on."

"Vegas just collapsed around us. I think it's understandable she's a little on edge."

"Just be careful who you trust, is all I'm saying."

"And does that include you? Am I supposed to trust you?"

K raised an eyebrow. "After what we went through in San Fran? I'd have thought I'd earned a place in your heart."

Terre smiled. "That's why I'm here. To check up on you."

"What do you think is happening here, exactly?"

Terre paused, unsure of how to answer the question. What *did* he think was happening? That K had buckled under the pressure of San Francisco?

No, if Terre was being honest, he thought the Agency's intel was faulty; that they were wrong about K's motives.

But before he vocalized it, Terre realized that he wanted to hear it from the programmer himself.

"Fredricks called me just after the power went out; told me Intel's been tracking us both."

"And that surprised you?"

"Not really. But he told me you were out here. The

Agency thinks you caused the outage; that you've done something to the bots to make them turn on us again."

"*Hah!* And you thought there was a shred of credibility to that?"

"No, and neither did Fredricks."

K raised an eyebrow. "You're kidding?"

"I'm not."

"Why did you *really* come out here, Terre? I thought you were done with all this shit."

"I *was* done! You think I wanted to be chased by another faction of robot soldiers? Narrowly escape a terrorist attack on my hotel? To crawl out into the desert to find your pasty ass?"

"So why? What's your angle?"

"Fredricks got authorization to send me out here instead of a kill squad."

"After everything we just went through?" K scoffed. He slammed an open palm against the steering wheel. "*Damn it!*" he screamed. "They seriously think I'm going to turn around and unleash Armageddon? What the hell?"

Unsure if his friend had indeed become unhinged, Terre pressed his back against the door and lifted his hands outwardly toward him. "Easy now, buddy. We'll get this straightened out. But I need to know *exactly* what is going on. Why are *you* out here?"

K exhaled sharply and rolled his eyes before letting out a grunt.

"It's some dude at a desk looking at facts and figures," Terre said. "Fill me in so we can set them straight."

"It'll be easier if I show you. We're going there anyway."

"The kids the bots have taken?" Annika piped up from the back seat. "How are they involved?"

K's gaze was locked on the road before them. "It's all connected. Again, it'll be easier if you can see it for yourselves."

"K?" Terre pressed. "The vigilante scientists. The abandoned town. Fredricks told me something's been going on here for weeks."

"Yeah, and you didn't bother to ask why they didn't send a team in weeks ago? They pulled the National Defense units off the Dam before it happened. I'm not entirely sure why, but the military seems to be resigned to just let this happen."

"Let *what* happen?"

"You're going to have to wait. We're almost there."

Terre sighed but forced himself to be patient. He mulled over their brief conversation, K's words stewing around in his head.

"Why don't you trust Hailey, K? If it wasn't for her, I'd still be out walking in the desert."

"You'd be better off in the desert, Terre." K shook his head. "The CIA isn't interested in stopping this thing, and I think your friend's only interested in stopping me, but that's not the same thing."

"I wish you'd tell me what you're doing."

"The same thing I was doing in San Francisco, but this time, I had to take matters into my own hands. You know how the government was handling things."

"You mean, they weren't?"

"Exactly. The bots weren't going to fix themselves." K shook his head again. "The Guardian Program wasn't a fix at all, and I said as much six weeks ago. It's been active this whole time. The programming kept the attacks at bay, but otherwise the bots have been active, just not in the way you'd expect. After I took leave, I realized I couldn't be the one responsible for letting the whole thing go, so I called up some of my buddies at NASA. Like I told you before, they'd worked on the original code with me, as well as a few aspiring students who were top of their class. They'd seen the Sentinels at Berkley, they had a sense of what was at stake, so a few agreed to help. They've been with me ever since."

"What happened to Boulder City, anyway? I haven't ever seen anything like it. Other than wartime coverage."

"We're in wartime, pal." K sighed. "Maybe the last war humanity ever fights."

The comment gave Terre pause. It was something he intrinsically knew to be true, but he hadn't taken the time to stop and consider it.

The end of everything.

Terre rubbed the spot on his shoulder where the nanos had healed his bullet wound. What did that mean for him and K? How far could the nanos protect them? How much would he want to endure?

"What about your role? Why are you and your team playing protectorate?"

"These are the bots *I* designed. Some of these folks were on my team, and they feel the same way. *Responsible.* Our work is being used to kill innocent people." K shook his head, momentarily closing his eyes. "It's too much. Chasing away the rest of the townspeople before the bots obliterated them was the least we could do. Keeping more from coming through? Well, that's in our best interest to keep prying eyes away."

Terre considered his friend's words. He understood the sentiment. How many people had died because of his own actions? Isn't that why he'd brought Annika along?

He decided it was time to change the subject. "So, what happened?"

"Part of it will be hard to grasp without the context of what I'm about to show you. At first, nobody noticed that the AI had taken over complete control of the Dam. The operation was already mostly automated, and the only humans there most of the time, besides tours, were the National Guard, protecting the power grid. Boulder City was the first to notice the tourists had quit coming. The buses were going through, but they weren't stopping."

The rocky terrain continued to pass them by. The red rock hills had always seemed otherworldly to Terre, like they were an alien landscape on a far-off planet, and he couldn't help but be struck by the irony: they made for one hell of a fitting backdrop for a robot attack.

A sign to turn off for the Hoover Dam came and went, but K kept driving.

"Where are we going?" Terre asked.

"The Arizona side of the canyon."

Terre nodded, as though the comment meant anything to him. "Why here?" he asked. "This can't be the epicenter of what's happening."

"The Guardians need a power source."

Terre raised an eyebrow. "'The Guardians?' What the hell are you talking about?"

"Do you remember the original specification for the bots? The orbs and the Keeper bots the Sentinels were based on?"

"Keepers?" Annika piped up. "So, what Terre said is true? If the Sentinels have malfunctioned, the Keepers have become killing machines, too?" Her voice trembled with worry.

"That's *not* what I said!" Terre interjected. "I said they were designed from the same model."

"Not exactly," K clarified, ignoring Terre. "The Keepers, like the orbs, were designed to preserve the Mars colony. We originally designed them to protect the colonists from the inhospitable planetary conditions surrounding their biodome. They have one function: to keep the colonists safe."

"Right, but the military's gone and fucked that up," Terre said. "We've been through all this. I thought our upload of the Guardian Program was supposed to revert these things back to factory default?"

The vehicle turned a bend and the Bypass Bridge opened

up before them, crossing the state line between Nevada and Arizona and overlooking the Boulder River. The Hoover Dam waited below them.

Annika pointed out the vehicle's window. "Are those orbs?"

Terre had to strain around Kristopher to see, but he was able to make out several floating spheres circling the dam.

"They are," K said, not offering any further details.

The Arizona landscape across the bridge shouldn't have looked any different from the rocky terrain on the Nevada side, but the landscape was unfamiliar somehow. The tops of the hills were smoother, the hills not as rough as Terre's memories of the place.

A stark realization gripped him as he pieced together what K had been alluding to.

"They're terraforming the terrain," he said. "The bots are acting like they would if they were on Mars. As they were designed to be."

"That doesn't sound so bad," Annika said.

"If that was all that was happening, it wouldn't be," K replied.

"The unknowns," Terre stated. "The upload did exactly what you thought it would—resetting the original units—but the bots are still outside of our control, so they're terraforming the landscape as though they're on Mars. The Sentinels and Onyx were created for military use. Different purpose, programmed to fight, but equally outside of our control."

"That's about the gist of it, but something else has gone screwy with the program. The Sentinels' operating systems have integrated the strands of code designating the outside world as hostile. In effect, they're running a bastardization of the Guardian Program. They've been designed to destroy anything hostile."

"What do you mean, 'the outside world?' Outside of what?"

The highway crested another rise, and the effects of the terraforming became clearer. A large swath of land had been stripped flat. In place of mountainous, rocky terrain was a smooth platform of rock populated by dozens of buildings. They were plain and flat structures that Terre recognized as having been 3D-printed from the very dirt they had been constructed on.

"They're rebuilding the Mars settlement." Terre spoke the realization aloud, answering his own question. Terre had only seen footage of the structures the bots had been building. "That entire settlement is surrounded by a giant force field, exactly how far is this going to go?"

"I hope we don't have to find out," K replied.

Terre pulled his gaze away from the landscape and to the rearview mirror. Hailey and Becky were still following them. He wondered what Hailey thought of the scenes that greeted them on the otherwise inhospitable terrain.

"But that still doesn't fully explain where you come in, K," Terre said. "There has to be more to your involvement than just trying to shut down a massive construction project?"

K studied Terre as though searching the man for the answer. "You're right. I've been trying to fix where I went wrong. Trying to shut down the bots entirely."

"Is that possible? Do you still have network rights?"

"Accessing the network is now impossible. We made sure of that when our upload failed."

Terre gritted his teeth, biting back the grief of his own shortcomings.

"Stop that!" K barked, reading his expression. "Blaming yourself isn't going to solve anything. You can deal with your guilt later."

"So, what, then? Why'd you come out here? If you're locked out of the network, what are you shutting down?"

"The entire power grid. If you haven't noticed, the bots' OS has infiltrated the public networks. Self-driving cars, electricity, everything from library cards to video games are now under the control of the Guardian Program."

All Terre could do was blink as he tried to process the information. Being locked out of the military's system was one thing, but being without access to the automated public systems was catastrophic. Nothing these days, from watering crops, to filling potholes, to stocking shelves at the grocery store, was achieved without AI integration.

Everything is automatic.

"I need to hack into the system and do what the government isn't willing to do."

With all the information now laid out before him, Terre was instantly on board. They needed to act. Every moment the bots were left unchecked, they strengthened their position, unquestioningly following their programming without any fail-safe parameters to protect human life.

"Couldn't we just blow the turbines?"

"Possibly," K answered. "But even if I wanted to, there are multiple problems in doing so. Even if we could get past the security bots and systems, there are multiple turbines on either side of the dam. Each side has seven or eight. I don't even know where I'd start in getting enough explosives to take them all out at the same time. We would have to lay out the explosives on each side and detonate them simultaneously. If we only struck one side, the security systems would completely lock out the other. And all that aside, it would only be a local fix. There are dozens of fail-safes that would kick in if the plant generator failed. It would slow things down, but we need a full stop."

"So, what's the plan, then?"

"You're not going to like it."

Chapter Nineteen

Annika

The settlement didn't look like much, but its intent was clear, both rudimentary and technologically advanced at the same time. Bots hovered past what appeared to be the foundations of squat homes and apartments, all close enough to the dam to glean power from it, yet sprawling into the Arizona desert. Lake Mead sat to its north, stretching out to the horizon, supplying hydroelectricity, irrigation, and water to much of the country for over a hundred years.

The buildings the automated machines had constructed were a marvel but considering that there wasn't a human hand involved in their creation, it sent chills down Annika's spine.

The start of a revolution.

Annika breathed in deep. The dry desert air scratched her nose, throat, and lungs. Ten miles behind them, bots had destroyed a city; now, before her, it appeared as though the machines were creating a new one.

Annika didn't pretend that she understood everything Terre and Kristopher had discussed—she was no computer engineer—but she did grasp that whatever the two geeks had done to stop the war machines in San Francisco had now created this reality. To Annika's understanding, it was a reality where bots seemed both at odds with their intended design and yet worked toward their own skewed goals. She also grasped that the foundations of what she saw around her would be the end of everything she had ever known if Klein's plan didn't work.

And they still didn't even know what that plan really was.

"It's beautiful, isn't it?" Hailey had snuck up behind Annika, causing her to jump.

"You startled me," Annika said, sticking her thumbs in her pockets as she surveyed the construction. "My sister is down there somewhere. Beauty or horror, it doesn't matter until I've got her back. If we're going down there, let's go."

"Maybe your sister is meant for bigger things. Part of the new order."

"And what would you know of order?" Kristopher closed the door of the truck before approaching.

"I know there's more order in machine than man. More structure in tech than in flesh."

Annika put her hands up, trying to stop the arguing before it became more heated. "I'm sorry, but I don't understand half of what you folks have been talking about." She realized, if nothing else, that Kristopher and Hailey opposed each other. She didn't care why, but she refused to get caught in the middle. "I didn't come here on any secret mission to stop the bots. I just want to get Cheyenne and wait for everything to go back to normal."

"I think what Hailey's saying," Terre said, approaching, "is that we don't know if things will be normal for a very long time. Maybe not ever again."

Annika gritted her teeth. "*I'm* saying I don't care. It's time to get my sister out of there."

"We're not going down there," K said. "I said I'd show you where she was, but our work is at the Dam."

Annika's heart sank. Part of her had hoped they'd stick around long enough to help. She quickly shook off the disappointment. She had already made her decision. It was time to follow through.

"But I'd prefer not to go in there alone. Every time I've pushed into the fire, it's ended in disaster, but I won't give up on Cheyenne." Determination burned in her belly, blazing like the heat from the furnace she was considering jumping into. It might be suicide to go on her own, but she hadn't gone once before when her gut told her to, and Annika had regretted it ever since. She'd rather get burned than live with the regret of letting Cheyenne down as well.

"Well, I'm going with you." Becky positioned herself firmly beside Annika with a grin. "You know I am."

Annika nodded.

"The bots will kill you," Kristopher said confidently. "Your sister will be safer there than anywhere else before we can shut them down."

Annika couldn't help but catch the dangerous glint that flashed in Hailey's eye.

Be careful who you trust.

"And if you can't? I'm not afraid of dying, but I'm terrified of living with regret."

Terre's eyes locked onto hers, and she saw it; saw it as clearly as if it were written on his forehead. *Regret.* The same guilt that had plagued her every night since her parents' death, the same shame that had ripped through her a million times, was there in Terre's eyes, but his seemed deeper. She couldn't imagine the devastation of losing a child; the guilt of letting those in your care down. She knew her parents weren't her responsibility, but their deaths still haunted her. The pain Annika saw in Terre's eyes was the pain she feared would consume her if she let Cheyenne down.

Terre let out a sigh. "All right. I'm in. But we need to be quick. We need to give K the time he needs."

Hailey shook her head. "No way. You were sent here on a mission, Hoffmann, and there's no damn way I'm going to let you walk away from it. You can't go wandering off to save some teenager."

Terre's face turned a shade of purple. "First of all, Hailey, I didn't want to come out here to begin with. You might remember I gave Fredricks a hundred reasons why he shouldn't be sending me out here. So, don't start talking to me about *duty.*"

Hailey crossed her arms, leaning back at the sudden change in tone.

"Second, I still don't know why you were scoping me out in that bar. You claim it was to make sure I did my job. Well, look, I'm here. My mission was to find K; to make sure he wasn't the one behind the latest wave of attacks. And, look, here he is. He's going to show me what he's up to. What do you want me to do?"

"I want to see *exactly* what Klein is up to," Hailey said, ignoring the man standing right next to Terre. "The fate of the nation is at stake here! You don't take the word of the enemy who claims to hide nothing; you inspect their facility. And I thought I'd made it painfully clear that if you won't take responsibility, *I* will. We need to accompany him to the facility and ensure his story checks out."

Annika couldn't tell whether Terre was considering Hailey's words or suppressing an eye-roll. Either way, the afternoon sun was beating down on them, and she was ready to move. Her soiled blouse was already damp with sweat, and Terre's newly gained flannel shirt wasn't doing him any favors in the heat, either. It was clear the gear she had helped Hailey lift from Harold and Frank had been purposed for the cool mountain evenings, not an afternoon in the sun.

Terre's eyes found her own again. The tiredness behind his stare betrayed the youth the rest of his face mimicked. Somehow, the man simultaneously seemed older and younger than he really was. Annika could almost see him push down the pain, the guilt she had felt a connection to only mere moments before, as if he was intentionally hardening himself by what she could only imagine was obligation.

Then the eyes softened again, and Annika could tell Terre knew there was only going to be one path for her. And he couldn't disagree with her decision.

A shiver passed through her in the seemingly never-ending moments before Terre spoke. The fear of venturing into the unknown yet again to find Cheyenne was so much more intimidating than it had been the day before. Yesterday, she'd left the Convention Center, determined to be by her sister's side, and there had been no hesitation that she'd go it alone. Even if Becky had left her at that point, Annika would have made the quest solo.

Yesterday, it felt as though nothing could have stopped her. But after wave upon wave of militarized bots, an emerging terrorist faction, a few explosions, car chases, and drone strikes, the path to what she desired most in the entire world didn't seem as easy to conquer. Annika felt as though she were nothing more than a small naive farm girl in the middle of a big, wide world of danger. No amount of grit and determination to keep her and her sister together had prepared her. Hell, *nothing* could have prepared her for what the last twenty-four hours had wrought.

And now Annika would have to venture into the lion's den.

"I don't suppose you'd be willing to wait until we've had a look at K's work?" Terre asked.

Annika sighed. The man understood her need to rescue her sister, but Terre didn't seem to want to let *her* go, either.

"How many times do I have to tell you?" Hailey crossed her arms, growing more irritable by the minute. "She's not your damn rescue project. From what K said, there are other kids out there. What are you going to do? Save them all?"

Annika could see the wheels turning as Terre considered the weight of Hailey's words.

"If I can," he answered, before turning back to Annika. "But as much as I'd love to come with you, Hailey's right. I think K might be on to something, but he needs a solid plan. If there's a way I can help to put a stop to this, we can worry about the kids later. But I sure as hell understand your need to find your sister."

Annika nodded, fighting back tears. She turned to Becky, who simply gave her a nod before putting a comforting hand on Annika's shoulder. The woman's quiet but affirming presence calmed the nerves that churned in Annika's gut.

Now, she had to choose. Should she wait for the tech experts to do whatever it was they needed to do before going in? What if they failed? They already had once.

She could go in, risk it all, and fail, or she could wait, do nothing, and fail anyway. She couldn't live with that. She couldn't live with not trying.

Annika turned to Kristopher, who had seemed content leaning against his truck for the entire exchange. "Where can I find her?"

"If the bots have her, she'll be in the settlement. You'll have to find a way to get in undetected, which, considering the surveillance drones, will be nearly impossible. You're lucky the Sentinels are currently all occupied destroying the cities, but that doesn't mean the bots you'll see there aren't deadly. They might not have been designed for combat, but that doesn't mean the military didn't equip some of the orbs with weapons systems."

"Orbs?" Becky chimed in. "Do they have Onyx units there?"

Annika's head swam with memories of news reports highlighting the giant black balls firing upon structures in the city of San Francisco. The same orbs now hovered above Vegas. Their attack had been stifled, for reasons even Terre didn't seem to understand, but their presence alone was still making a mark.

"They're not Onyx," Kristopher replied. "These units are closer to the drones we developed with NASA. Smaller, and in a variety of colors. Most are silver or gray, and we designed white orbs for the MedCenters. You're more likely to come across those in the settlement. Just bear in mind they're still dangerous."

"Have you been inside?" Annika pressed. "How might I get through to where they're holding Cheyenne?"

The programmer shook his head. "My goal has been to end this. If you ask me, those kids are in the safest place in the world right now. If the bots are herding them to these fake Mars stations, the coding for preservation of life remains intact. It's the disconnect between the colony bots and the military units that our upload wasn't able to bridge."

"What about the rest of your team?" Hailey asked. "What are they doing? Where are they now?"

Kristopher turned to Terre. "Is she always this bossy?"

Annika swore Terre was doing his best not to crack a smile. "She's driven."

"That's one word for it," Kristopher scoffed. "Some of my people are going to stick around here; keep the transients moving. The rest are down at the dam. We'll meet them there. And you can get your *proof.*" He gave a sidelong glance at Terre, his eyebrow raised.

It was quick and subtle, but Annika didn't miss his hand briefly brushing against his cloak, near his hip. Kristopher was armed. Was he preparing in case Hailey didn't like what she would find?

For all the shade and suspicion he cast on Hailey, Annika wondered how much they could really trust the programmer. Perhaps Hailey had a reason to be as curt as she had been.

"Can I talk to you before I go?" she asked Terre, her eyes unconsciously bouncing between Kristopher and Hailey. "Alone?"

Chapter Twenty

Cheyenne

Cheyenne was exhausted. The machines had marched through the night, not stopping, not even slowing their pace. Her feet ached. Her sneakers hadn't been made for trekking through the desert. Their baby blue hue was now faded and dingy beneath layers of dust and sweat. Perhaps there were even a few spots of blood where blisters had burst.

Ember had marched beside her for the entire journey, and still Cheyenne hadn't been told anything, other than to keep walking. But the bots had given her food and water. Other bots flew far overhead, oblivious to their caravan moving across the desert. Or perhaps they didn't care.

Cheyenne couldn't say she had been mistreated, but wherever the bots were planning on taking her, they were moving with determination.

By the time they had finally stopped moving, it barely registered with Cheyenne that she was among buildings, bots, and other youths. Dozens, maybe more—maybe a *hundred*—all looking as annoyed, tired, and frustrated as she was.

A young boy and girl, possibly brother and sister, stood with their backs to a wall, holding hands.

"Where are we?" the boy asked. His striped *Iron Man* shirt was dirty and worn from the journey. "Where's Mom?"

His sister patted his arm as if to quiet him, her wide eyes roaming among the bots as though fearing punishment for her brother's words. "Quiet, Bentley!" she urged.

The caravan of bots Cheyenne had arrived with had dispersed. As she glanced around her, almost delirious with tiredness, she noticed the surrounding buildings appeared to be in various states of construction. Though simple, they appeared to be modern, and the soil had colored the buildings a light shade of red.

Cheyenne watched bricks being laid by a nearby machine and gradually realized that it was using soil to construct the dwellings. No need to bring in materials; the bots were building the structures from the ground beneath them.

"What is this place, Ember?" she asked. The Keeper had been silent for most of the trip.

"This will be your new home, Cheyenne."

Cheyenne's face contorted. She could have guessed a million things her Keeper might have told her, but *that* was definitely not on the list.

"Ember, that's not funny. Why did you bring me out here?"

Throughout the night, she couldn't help but continue to think Annika would find her. But when that hadn't happened, reality had slowly begun to creep in. Ember clearly had a reason for leading her away from the city.

At first, Cheyenne had been angry—the bot had taken her against her will—but as the night wore on, she came to realize the severity of what was happening. The pieces came together as the world around them fell apart.

Ember was protecting her from the destruction of the city.

The only worry that plagued Cheyenne's mind now was where Annika had ended up. Ember either didn't know or didn't want to say. The bot's primary concern was getting her to safety; Cheyenne had spent more than enough time with the machine to know that. And she knew that safety would be what Annika would want for her as well.

But that didn't mean she didn't worry about her sister.

Cheyenne fought to hold back the tears; to hold back the panic from what she currently faced. Perhaps Annika was dead.

"We will protect you here."

"Who is 'we?'"

"The Guardians."

"Ember, you're not making any sense. Who are the Guardians?"

"The world is under attack. This place will be safe. The Guardians will protect you here."

Under attack.

The explosions. The panic in the city. The desperate drivers trying to break out of their cars. The bots with laser guns, firing on the citizens in the streets. The drones flying overhead, diving into homes and buildings as Cheyenne had followed another group of automated bots deep into the night.

"Where's Annika? Can't you protect her, too?"

Ember stood silent for a moment, the lights on her frame pulsing gently, as though thinking about the query.

"Annika is not authorized."

"Ember, I can't leave her. I'm all she has."

"The wars have started. It is no longer safe."

"Wars? What war? What are you talking about?"

"The war between machine and man," Ember replied. "Humans have created the mechanisms of war. They will destroy everything if we do not intervene and protect humanity."

Cheyenne, unable to comprehend what Ember was saying, backed up and lost her footing, tripping over in the dirt. Before she could process the fall, Ember's arm was beneath her, catching her, saving her from harm once again.

"I am here for your protection," the bot replied.

The bot *had* always been there, but so had Annika. Her sister had done what she could, at least. But if the world was ending … That meant everything would change.

Annika had left Cheyenne in Ember's care more often than she'd liked. The bot had been her best friend in so many ways, despite having no personality to speak of.

Various types of bots both flew around them and stood with the other youths. Children of all ages, wide-eyed and frightened, huddled together as they tried to determine if their new reality was safe. There were other Keepers here, too, and orbs and other bots, all tending to the various needs of the refugees brought in tow. It was a foreign feeling to no longer be the only kid with a bot. Before the white-paneled bots had started killing everyone, Cheyenne had never seen any other bots like Ember before.

Most of the other kids were gathered in the center of whatever village this was, appearing more bored than anything else, though some of the younger ones were listless, crying, and yelling.

For all intents and purposes, this appeared to be a place where Cheyenne would no longer be an oddball for having a bot as a friend.

This will be your new home, Cheyenne.

Images of armed bots marching into the city had all but evaporated. This place was safe. But there was more to it than that.

It felt as though this was somewhere Cheyenne might actually belong.

Chapter Twenty-One

Terre

"How much do you trust him?"

Annika's question slapped Terre in the face. It was reminiscent of the first time he had sworn in front of his mother. Like then, he wasn't so much hurt as he was shocked by the sudden swing.

Terre fought to keep his gaze on Annika. Hailey had accused him of trying to be her savior; to keep her from harm because he hadn't been able to save his own family. He wondered how much of that was true. He wondered how much of it *mattered*. Was it so bad to want to help someone? To keep another family from being torn apart?

Annika's question would have seemed ridiculous, a grim joke, had it not been for the seriousness of her expression. He would have expected a similarly cold line of questioning from Hailey, but he thought he had done enough to build Annika's trust by now.

"When you go through what Kristopher and I did ..." Terre shook his head and ran a hand over his coarse black hair. He didn't know how to finish the thought. They had been through not one, but *two* harrowing bombings. They had worked together to put an end to the robot attacks. And suddenly, everyone was suspicious of the programmer's intentions. Fredricks and Hailey were bad enough, but Annika barely knew the man. In the hour since they'd encountered K and his band of nerd warriors, had there really been enough time for her to form suspicions? Sure, K seemed a little erratic. That might be enough to set off someone's internal alarm bells, but was it really enough to warrant genuine concern?

How much do you trust him?

Hailey had a valid point about double-checking what K's team was up to. There was no sense in blindly putting too much faith in the man's words, especially if the Agency had their suspicions. Especially if Hailey was authorized to shoot first and ask questions later.

Hailey had obviously bought into whatever story the CIA had concocted.

But Annika had no vested interest, no preconceived notions. She had nothing to go on but Terre's word, and the hour she had spent with Kristopher.

How much do I trust him? A hell of a lot more than I trust Hailey.

"K helped stop one of the biggest threats ever seen on American soil. The largest attack since Pearl Harbor." He couldn't resist, and Terre looked back to where the programmer stood, still leaning against the truck, his arms crossed, and his sunglasses perched on his nose. Kristopher appeared to be surveying the burgeoning bot settlement in the distance; the newly constructed group of buildings where Annika's sister was likely being held.

Terre couldn't help but admit that something about K had changed in the past six weeks; something he had trouble putting his finger on, but not anything that rang any alarm bells. If anything, K was more confident, more assured of himself and his purpose. Maybe he was a bit more of a smart-ass, with a swagger that hadn't been present in San Francisco.

"He has a gun," Annika said, her voice lowered.

Terre nearly burst out laughing. "So do you! If he's been working on stopping renegade robots, I think he's entitled to arm himself."

"But that's just it! These bots are supposedly killing anyone they don't take into their care. You saw Boulder City! How has Kristopher and his crew managed to stay unscathed through all of this? You don't think that raises a few red flags?"

Annika was hissing out the last words, struggling to keep her voice quiet, the tendons in her neck stretched tight with the effort. The woman wasn't just concerned; K's involvement terrified her.

Could it be possible K was duping him? He didn't know the man prior to Guam, but … It just didn't add up. The man had been little more than a ball on the floor after the death of Ali, their chaperone in San Francisco that K had become smitten with in a matter of minutes. The poor agent was decapitated by a pane of glass that had been dislodged as the bots instigated their last wave of terror six weeks ago. Fredricks had sent the agent to fly the pair from San Francisco to Berkley, and her death had nearly ruined K. Terre just couldn't bring himself to believe that the same Kristopher Klein would suddenly about-face and unleash an army of bots upon the American people.

"I'll watch my back," Terre said. "But if I can't give K the benefit of the doubt, there's *nobody* I can trust."

A faint smile crept onto the woman's thin lips, as though he'd just said the most ridiculous thing possible. "You can trust *me*," she said. "For what it's worth."

Terre crossed his arms. "You just met me. You don't owe me anything."

Annika didn't contain her laugh this time. It was high and

shrill, and not at all what Terre had expected her laugh to sound like. The genuine guffaw encompassed her entire body, as though, in that moment, it needed to release all the tension that had been building up over the course of the last day or so.

"You, sir," she said as she composed herself and the laughter faded, "you have saved my life *three* times in the past twenty-four hours. Despite all my protests, despite my bad decisions, despite everything within me wanting to rescue Cheyenne alone, you have come along and proven I am not the island I imagined myself to be. You have shown me that there are people willing to help, and that I need them."

Annika inhaled deeply, letting out a sigh as she closed her eyes. "I've needed *you*. More than I would ever have believed. So, thank you. I wouldn't have made it this far without your help."

She opened her eyes, tears now filling them.

Terre fumbled with the words to say to reciprocate. "And you've proven to me," he said, after what felt like several long moments, "that no matter how much I'd rather hide from this world, there are still those who need a hand."

He reached out and the slender woman fell into his arms, hanging on as though he were an old friend she knew she wouldn't see for a very long time.

"You've got this," he said reassuringly. "I wish I could go with you, but I know you're strong enough to handle this alone." The woman deflated in his arms, as though the weight of the world had suddenly made its presence known on top of her shoulders. Terre was happy to help carry the burden, even if for just a few moments longer. "Cheyenne is lucky to have someone willing to fight so hard for her. There's not many who would do the same in your shoes."

Annika stepped back, her face creasing in confusion. "I'm just doing what anyone would do for their loved ones. I'm the only family she has."

"Sometimes, that's not enough," Terre said. *Sometimes we fail despite our best intentions.* "But c'mon, this isn't the end for us. Make sure you look for us once you've found her. If you can't find our vehicle on the way back to Boulder City, we'll meet you there. The hike will take a few hours, but it should be doable. Lay as low as you can, but hopefully we'll have put an end to these things before then."

Annika nodded and waved Becky over.

"If by chance one of us doesn't make it, thank you for everything."

"Likewise," Terre said.

Annika smiled before walking over to Becky and beginning their trek toward their destination.

"We need to move," Kristopher said, his eyes turning skyward. "We don't have much time."

"Much time?" Terre asked, trying to follow his gaze. "Much time until what?"

Nothing but blue sky rested above them. A single raven flew past, but otherwise Terre didn't see what had caught K's attention.

"War," K replied simply.

Providing no further explanation, the man jumped into his truck.

"K, I don't see what it is you…"

And then he did. Terre's eyes rested on the black dots, mere specks in the sky, flying in unison, as if a single unit. They had to be miles away, their destination somewhere west.

"They're headed for Vegas," Terre said. "There's dozens of them."

"They're the military's problem now," Hailey offered. She followed K's lead and stepped casually to the SUV.

"There's only one thing the military's going to do to stop that," Terre said. "And so far, they've expressed no interest in doing so."

"Maybe humanity's time at the top of the food chain has come to an end," Hailey commented.

"If we don't light the match before they get there, we'll be locked out completely," K said. "It won't matter what happens then. Get in, Terre. We've got to move."

"Wait! What's he talking about?" Hailey called out.

Terre was already halfway to the truck. "We'll fill you in once we're there!"

"Once we're where?"

Terre didn't respond; he had only a faint idea of what was going on himself.

"What happens once we get to the Dam?" he asked Kristopher as he shut the truck's passenger side door.

"There's a chance we're going to be able to manually override the system, but it's a long shot. And we'll only get one chance before the AI network realizes something's happening."

"I feel like we've done this before."

K laughed; a full belly laugh that felt both comforting and unnatural at the same time.

"What's really at stake here, K? Will this really work? The bots must have other ways of powering themselves."

"Not after this, they won't. I wish I could say we're doing anything but minimizing the damage at this point, but it seems like that's all we've been able to hope for from the beginning. The bots are going to knock us back a century's worth of development, no matter what, but I hope we can slow them down enough for humanity not to live in fear of robot overlords for the rest of our existence."

"How long will the bots be able to run without power?" Terre asked. "And is this something we're going to be able to flick back on once we're done?"

K gave Terre a dire look. "Not at all. We're going to overload the entire system."

Terre's mind struggled to comprehend the implications of what the programmer was saying. "What? Like blow the breaker?"

"In a manner of speaking."

Terre frowned. "Walk me through it."

"We're not just going to flip a switch and turn off the lights," K said. "I'm talking about a full black sky event. For this to work, we need to make sure the power *doesn't* come back on."

Terre held his breath as he considered K's words. For years, maybe decades, the fear of a national blackout had been something the government had been working to avoid. He didn't know where to start in asking questions. There were hundreds he was trying to wrap his head around, never mind ask.

"We have to send a surge through the grid," K continued, sensing Terre's uncertainty. "We don't just knock out the power; we send a rush of electricity that kills this grid and then sends a domino effect into nearby systems. It'll be lights out across the country."

Terre eyed the programmer skeptically. "For how long?"

"Best case scenario, it would take the country a year to get the power grid working again. Unfortunately, we're still going to have the bots to contend with for a month or two before their reserve power's completely depleted."

Terre did his best to keep his mouth from hitting the floor of the truck, but he imagined he failed miserably. "Damn it, K! You're talking about sending the US back to pre-industrial times."

Kristopher was talking about national terrorism on a scale that hadn't ever been seen. It would make exploding a few hotel rooms seem like a mild inconvenience. Maybe Hailey wasn't being as paranoid as Terre had imagined.

How much do you trust him?

"Do you know how many people will die if the power's knocked out for a year?" Terre pressed.

"There will be a lot more dead if we don't do this!" K snapped.

"K, I'm all for the American spirit, but people won't know how to survive without electricity. Winter is just around the corner. Tens, maybe *hundreds* of thousands, will freeze or starve to death."

"I've run the numbers, Terre. There won't be an American city or town that isn't obliterated by these bots. Maybe a few pockets of humanity will survive, but we'll be scavengers for the rest of our existence. If we pull this off, at least there's a possibility we can one day rebuild."

Terre sighed, putting his hands behind his neck, trying to come to terms with what K was presenting as the *best* case scenario. "Aren't there measures in place to prevent a surge from happening? Backup systems? Surge protectors? Power grid disruption should be something the country is prepared for."

K lifted an eyebrow. "You'd be surprised. All current measures in place are to prevent an *outside* attack on the grid. There's nothing to stop us from creating a surge from the inside."

"I dunno, K. There's a lot of automation along the chain. If one piece sees the surge coming, I can't see there not being a fail-safe."

"We don't have time to get into all the logistical details," K said. "Trust me. I haven't just been sitting around on my ass for the past two weeks, waiting for all hell to break loose. I've been sorting out this problem. I wish we had more time, but it seems Armageddon is here. It's not a perfect plan, but it *should* work."

"And if it doesn't?"

"Then we're all dead."

Chapter Twenty-Two

Annika

"So, what's the plan?" Becky asked.

The two women had stumbled across more rocks, boulders, sand, and shrubs than Annika believed she had ever seen, but it hadn't taken long before they'd found themselves overlooking the buildings the bots had constructed. Annika was still in awe that they'd gone up overnight.

The rocky terrain surrounding the makeshift village appeared void of any natural life. There were no trees or grasses to speak of, and the few shrubs nearby were barely more than dried-out sticks jutting from the dirt. It made the work of the robots stick out like a sore thumb, and it was clear their work wasn't done yet.

Machinery still streamed into the area in mile-long caravans stretching out into the desert. The lines included the construction equipment Annika had seen making its exodus from Las Vegas the day before. Pieces of the events from the past few days were finally falling into place.

The small, squat buildings were coming together before her eyes. It was mesmerizing to watch the automated bots printing their walls, continuing construction two and three stories high, but the purpose the machines had for this development was still murky. Annika was only vaguely familiar with Cyber Dynamics' Mars terraforming program —it had been one of the biggest NASA contracts ever awarded. She recalled seeing something on social media about 3D-printing structures on the planet, to save on the expensive venture of shipping supplies to the otherwise barren world.

And now, according to Kristopher—*if* they could trust him—the bots had taken that same programming and were applying it to printing buildings in the Arizona desert. If she couldn't see it with her own eyes, Annika didn't know if she would have believed it.

And somewhere among the mass of malfunctioning machines, her sister sat within their grasp.

I hope.

The startling realization came to her in that moment. What if her sister wasn't here? What if the entire day had been a waste, and her sister was instead sitting inside the arena with the other evacuees?

"Anni?" Becky pressed. "Are you okay?"

Shaking off her racing thoughts, Annika realized she hadn't responded to her friend's initial question. "As okay as I can be, heading into this mess. And I don't have a plan. Let's just see if we can find where the kids are being kept without getting our heads blown off."

Annika had meant it as a joke, but her words landed flat. Both women were acutely aware they could very well be walking to their deaths.

"You know I don't expect you to do this, right, Becks? You barely wanted to come to Las Vegas, never mind run headfirst into a viper's nest of murderous bots. I won't hold it against you if you want to stay back with Terre and Hailey."

"You keep giving me outs, but I'll keep refusing them.

Quit second-guessing my decision. I'm coming with you. End of story."

Annika tried to push down the guilt, trying to shove off the burden she thought she must be.

"The whole reason you came to Vegas was because of me," Annika said. "You didn't even want to leave Canada. It seems you were right to want to stay home. Not only did I bring you out of your comfort zone, but I also brought you to the epicenter of the apocalypse."

"How long have we known each other?" Becky asked. "Ten? Twelve years? Do you remember when we were sixteen? I was about to get into that vehicle with Ben Peterson the night of the party by the river?"

Ben Peterson, the hometown hockey hero. It had been so long since Annika had thought of him. The kid had the best shot on goal record Saskatoon had seen in decades, maybe ever. It seemed like another lifetime ago, but she remembered the guy.

"A real asshole," she said.

"Yeah. You knew he was. You grabbed me and pulled me out of his truck, and I gave you a black eye for your trouble."

"I couldn't blame you. I would have done the same to you if you'd tried to kill my first ever hook-up."

Becky shook her head. "I would have been one of a dozen other girls he assaulted that summer. When his behavior came to light, he lost his NHL prospects, his college scholarships, everything. It didn't matter that I clocked you and didn't talk to you for two months after. You stepped in and were the friend I needed."

"I could have done without the black eye that summer," Annika huffed. "But what's your point?"

Becky smiled. "You've always had my back." She rested a hand on Annika's shoulder. "And I'll always have yours."

Annika couldn't help but grimace at some of the thoughts she'd had over the past day or so. She'd almost abandoned

Becky in the stairwell of the Grand Kawa in her haste to find Cheyenne.

"Becky, I really appreciate that, but you know Cheyenne is my number one priority. If I have to choose between her or you, I …"

"You'd save her." Becky finished the sentence so that she didn't have to. "If it makes you feel any better, if I had to choose between you and Cheyenne, I'd pick her, too."

Becky equipped a grin, and Annika couldn't help catching the smile.

"You're damn right you would." She chuckled. "Do you think I'd ever let you hear the end of it if you didn't?"

Annika had meant it as a light-hearted jab, but the reality of what they were heading into must have hit Becky hard. Her eyes suddenly grew distant as she surveyed the developing town they were approaching.

"Hopefully neither one of us will need to make that call," Becky said.

Annika let the statement hang. "Come on," she said. "We should keep moving."

"What do you suppose the point of this is?" Becky asked. "A moat?"

They had made it to the outskirts of the bots' claimed territory. Now, only a couple hundred yards remained between Annika and Becky and the buildings. Orbs buzzed above the makeshift village, though they had yet to concern themselves with the pair's arrival.

Now, all that stood between Annika, Becky, and Cheyenne was a deep trench that had been dug into the earth, seemingly six feet, both wide and deep. The ditch was clearly artificial, cut into the earth with square corners and straight walls aligned either side. The length of the path disappeared to the horizon. Whatever it was going to be, it was clearly meant to encircle the bots' efforts—and it was going to be massive.

"I dunno," Annika said. "But we've got to find a way to cross it."

With everything that had transpired over the past day, a trench dug in the middle of the desert was hardly the strangest, nor the deadliest, obstacle they'd faced. It was barely something that should have given them pause, but besides the reddened alien landscape, it felt as though they truly had to cross a boundary into another world.

The two women approached the lip of the trench. It wouldn't be difficult to traverse.

"We could probably jump across," Becky said.

"Maybe *you* could," Annika said. "I wouldn't be able to jump that far. And even if I thought I could, I wouldn't want to risk it. If we misjudge it and twist an ankle, that's it. There's no way I could carry you back to the city."

They were now close enough to whatever the artificial intelligence was constructing that they could hear the sounds accompanying the build: the whirring of equipment; the beeping of machinery; the grinding of gears as computerized systems worked to lift dirt and rock and in and out of the worksites.

However, other than the occasional orb that zipped into view in the distance, there were no bots to be seen. Cliffsides or buildings obscured the crux of the activity. It wouldn't take them long to reach the heart of the new community, if Annika could call it that.

She moved to climb down the dip in the earth.

"Wait!" Becky hissed and grabbed Annika's arm, pulling her away from the crevice. "What are those things?"

Annika froze and did a double take at the structure she had been about to descend into. It took her a moment for her eyes to adjust to the shadows before she saw the potential hazards. A series of devices, constructed from metal, protruded from the earth's surface within the trench. They were pyramid-shaped mechanisms that stood half the height of the walls on either side of them, repeated every few dozen feet.

"There are dozens of them," Annika said. "And it looks like they stretch the entire length of the ring. What in the world are they?"

Becky gave her a bewildered shrug. "Your guess is as good as mine. Maybe a security system? Either way, I don't think we want to climb through there."

The black metal devices stood silent, their alien presence mocking her, guarding the path that led to the one thing she wanted more than anything else. They were so close. Annika couldn't accept that she had come this far, only to be stopped now.

What if the blocks weren't a security system? What if they were benign? There might have been another way around, but it would take them far out of their way to find it. And what if there was no other way across? How far were they willing to walk to find out?

The pylons certainly looked intimidating enough to be weaponized. Not as sleek as the orbs or the Sentinels, their dark metal was coarse, with a base that pulsed with a blue-tinted light. Seemingly, the devices were built for function—and perhaps intimidation—rather than style.

There had to be a way to get through.

"Get ready to run," Annika said.

"Why?" Becky responded. "What are you planning?"

Her friend had barely gotten the words out as Annika reached down to the earth below her and picked up a small rock. She wound up and released the projectile.

It flew toward the ditch in slow motion, and Annika could do nothing more than hold her breath and watch it spin in midair before landing on the pylon below.

It hit the device with the ping of rock upon metal. Annika held her breath, the silence of the mid-afternoon desert palatable. Even the distant machinery seemed to still.

Annika counted the seconds and waited until she reached thirty before she let her breath go. With hesitant relief, she turned to Becky. "Maybe they're turned …"

She didn't have time to finish the sentence before the pylon erupted. A burst of blue light filled the immediate vicinity of the trench, just over halfway to the next pylon on either side. More light shot up from the top of the device, firing hundreds of feet into the air in an arc over the settlement and the desert beyond.

The display lasted a few endless seconds before winking out again, the light dissipating into the sky and earth as if it had never revealed itself. And once again, the desert was silent.

Annika froze. She had launched the rock out of sheer desperation, with no real thought as to how it would play out. Perhaps, on some level, she'd expected the rock to disintegrate or be shot at. A beacon of light shooting out in all directions was not something she had envisioned.

"Well …" Becky swallowed. "If the bots didn't know we were here before, they certainly do now."

Chapter Twenty-Three

Annika

There was nowhere for Annika and Becky to hide, so they just ran.

An alarm sounded, its wailing intended to warn them, cautioning them to turn around, that the place they sought was too dangerous, but Annika couldn't pinpoint its source. The ringing reverberated so loudly in her head that it was almost as if it were coming from all directions. But instead, the alarm's call pushed them on, challenging Annika to keep going; to run faster; to do whatever it took to get into the robot construct and grab her sister.

Certain death lay ahead—but Annika couldn't quit now. How could she live with herself if she'd gotten this far and bailed at the last moment?

Annika had given up trying to talk Becky out of coming along. They were in this mess together. They were family. Becky was now putting her life on the line for Annika and Cheyenne, and Annika knew she would do the same for Becky if she was ever asked to.

If it matters after today.

More than a dozen silver orbs had left the nooks and crannies of the robot compound and were flying like enraged demons toward the spot where the pylon had erupted. It took all of Annika's effort not to slow down; not to try and take a closer look at the balls of tech hurtling toward them.

Less menacing than the Onyx, the spheres were still a sight to be feared. Annika guessed some of them were at least as tall as she was, while others might have been no bigger than a basketball. A glossy surface encapsuled each of them, reminding Annika of an old smartphone, as though their entire surface was a giant touchscreen.

As they grew closer, she could make out patterns of light on their surface. Bursts of red flashed and pulsed in sync with the alarm that deafened all around them.

Annika widened their path, hoping to veer out of the orbs' orbit, though she suspected they wouldn't be so easily fooled. The ragged landscape offered no source of relief. They had no options and little time.

They were running without cover, and Annika soon realized they were boxed in. The trench still ran parallel to them on their right. To their left was a cliff face, over which a fall would send them plummeting into the Colorado River. And it wasn't as if the cliff face was a sheer drop from which they'd be able to dive off into the waters below. Instead, doing so would mean, at best, rolling an ankle or, at worst, slamming headfirst into the red rock that climbed the river's banks. But it was still too steep for them to navigate down.

Becky slowed her pace beside Annika and then stopped.

Annika circled back to her friend. "What are you doing?"

Becky didn't even appear to be out of breath. Sweat glistened on her brow from the sun climbing in the sky, but other than heavy breathing, she seemed to be faring okay from the exertion.

"Why are we stopping?" Annika asked.

"Where exactly are we running to, Anni?" Becky's hands went to her hips as she breathed deeply. "There's nowhere to go."

Annika's eyes went to the spot where the pylon had erupted. It felt as though they had been running for ages, but in reality they'd covered little ground. Any bot that hovered overhead would see them. If the orbs hadn't spotted them already.

And the bots were growing expediently closer. It wouldn't be long before the two women would be forced to face them.

Becky's gaze was on the skyline, watching the orbs, scanning as if they might be able to make it to the buildings. As if that path would be any safer.

Any dreams of reaching the settlement dissipated as more orbs rose from its core, catapulting themselves sky-high in the blink of an eye. Their movements were so fast, Annika had to second-guess whether she had actually imagined them. These drones hovered in a cluster, probably a hundred feet in the air, before scattering in four compass-point directions.

Annika's stomach flipped as the original cluster continued to race toward them. Becky was right: there was nowhere to go.

Becky's fingers interlaced her own as they both stood, watching their impending doom. Neither of them spoke. There was nothing to say, so they'd stay strong in the moment. Annika looked at her friend. Becky's gaze was locked on the incoming threat. There were no tears in her eyes; only solid resolve. Annika was sure that Becky was at least as afraid as she was, but the woman didn't show it. If they were going to go down, they'd go down together.

It can't end like this, she thought. She couldn't leave Cheyenne with the bots, likely never knowing the fate of her big sister.

If you ask me, those kids are in the safest place in the world right now. K's words oddly gave Annika some slight comfort. She only hoped he was trustworthy.

The red pulsing lights on the orbs' surfaces increased in their intensity and rate of speed. Annika wasn't sure if they only appeared brighter because they were closer, but it didn't matter. She had seen the blasts from the Onyx. Even if these held only a fraction of the black giants' power, they'd be incinerated on the spot.

She held her breath as the orbs flew directly next to them; held it while they moved to hover over the pylon that had erupted minutes before; and released it when they zipped right past.

She stood there for a moment, dumbfounded, not quite ready to believe her eyes. There was no way the orbs hadn't detected them standing in the middle of the desert plain. She looked once more to Becky, who held the same bewildered stare of disbelief.

The orbs disappeared over the edge of the cliff, headed toward the Hoover Dam. Maybe they weren't after them at all? Perhaps triggering the pylon was a coincidence?

If that was the case, it wasn't difficult to put two and two together. The orbs were flying in the same direction Terre, Kristopher, and Hailey had gone.

"Do we count our lucky stars?" Becky asked. "I imagine we're not out of the woods yet."

"Do you think they're going after Terre? They went in the same direction."

"Who knows? But there's nothing we can do to help them. And that's a dozen fewer bots we have to avoid, not to mention the others that took off earlier." Becky put her hands behind her neck, scanning the skies as if they could return at any moment. "Still, that was creepy as hell. And I guess it doesn't matter if we're up against one of those things or a thousand. It'll only take a single laser bolt to kill us."

Annika's breath quickened for a moment. She knew the risks, and she knew it was her fault that Becky was heading into harm's way.

Becky must have noticed Annika's sudden change in demeanor. "I'm sorry, Anni. I didn't mean it like that. All I meant was not to let our guard down just because there's less of them. I don't want to be caught by surprise."

The tension melted a little from Annika's shoulders, but not entirely. There was still so much that could go wrong.

"Don't worry about it. You're right. And we can't stay out here. We still have to find a way in."

"Which way?" Becky asked.

Annika was grateful to be able to refocus on the task at hand. "I don't see a way to cross that trench. I think we're going to have to try to go through it again."

Becky let out a long, slow breath. "What about the pylons? What if they incinerate us if we try to get closer?"

"I don't see any other option. We'll cross at the center between the two pylons and be careful not to disrupt them as we go through. There was a small window of time between when the rock hit it and when it lit up. We step lightly, we go fast, and we pray they don't fire while we're inside."

Becky's gaze locked onto the trench, as though weighing what a venture through the ditch meant. "I don't like it," she said, "but you're right. There's no better option. Whatever this thing is, it seems to be dug for miles in either direction. Who knows where it ends? Or if it does. We could walk for hours and end up where we started."

The trench seemed to curve, if only slightly. "And in that time, those orbs could be back," Annika said. "So, let's do this."

Annika could have sworn the trench hadn't been so deep the first time they had surveyed it. It was going to take a concerted effort for them to scale down, never mind get back up on the other side.

She squatted down on the lip of the trench's maw, turning around so that her belly slid against the dirt as she inched herself down. It was just deep enough that she didn't quite trust herself to hop down. She inched down into the chasm, feet first, as far as her arms could reach, the dirt mixed with rock scraping her skin along the way.

Her hands clung to the edge as her feet dangled. Six feet had definitely been an underestimation; it was more like ten. Annika held on for a few moments before she let go, allowing herself to fall the last couple of feet. She stumbled as she landed but kept herself upright.

Becky was already down by the time Annika steadied herself, surveying the way up the other side.

"We maybe didn't think this through," she said.

"I think we'll be okay." Annika smiled, despite there being a part of her that wasn't so sure. The wall stood several feet above where either of them could comfortably reach. "Let me give you a boost. Once you're up, you can pull me."

Without waiting for a response, Annika bent down and faced the wall. "Get on my shoulders. Once I stand, you'll have enough height to pull yourself up."

Becky didn't argue. She took off her shoes, tossed them up and over the ledge, and stepped into Annika's cupped palms. She clamored up the side of the trench and pulled herself up the last few feet.

Grunts and groans accompanied Becky's effort, and Annika tried to give her an additional boost, pushing Becky's feet up with her hands to aid in the effort.

Becky rolled out of sight for a moment before turning around and reaching an arm into the ravine.

"Okay, Anni. Your turn!"

No sooner had Becky said the words than a familiar hum pulsed in the earth beneath her feet.

Chapter Twenty-Four

Terre

"These orbs don't seem too concerned about us. Should we be worried?"

Over ten years had passed since Terre had been here last, but he still couldn't help but feel a sense of awe as they crossed the Hoover Dam. Water rushed below, making their conversation hard to hear. Terre tried hard to listen to what K had to say, but it was hard to concentrate.

The occasional orb floating past didn't help matters. The bots weren't close, but Terre knew a little about the optical systems of the military drones, and he knew they'd probably be able to determine the thread count in his flannel shirt if they looked his way.

"My team was working to give us a window to work within. If they've done their job, we'll be able to get in without detection." Kristopher's coat flapped around him as they ran at a comfortable pace. "Once we generate the surge, though, all bets are off."

Hailey trailed behind the two specialists, seemingly annoyed at how the situation had progressed, but thankfully had resolved herself to keep her comments to herself, for now.

The Dam itself always felt majestic to Terre, the walled structure connecting the two canyon walls and bridging the gap between two states, its tan brickwork still holding strong after a hundred years, and likely to survive another thousand.

The parkade on the Nevada side of the monument loomed within the rise of the hillside as they approached the edge of the structure. A small building sat to their right; an old control center that had been converted into a museum ages ago. It was even older than the outdated systems that lay below them. Further ahead were a gift shop and restaurant that, until a few weeks ago, would have been serving overpriced burgers and fries.

Between the dam and the gift shop lay Monument Plaza, recording the date and time of the dam's construction, preserving its history in such a way that civilizations in the far future might understand, with a twenty-six-thousand-year celestial calendar.

Terre had previously thought little of the clues left in the plaza to potential future generations. Now it appeared that one day, they might provide some benefit. If civilization was to be completely wiped out, how much knowledge would be forever lost in the absence of tech?

They died to make the desert bloom.

The inscription marked remembrance of the workers who had perished during the dam's construction. Terre had memorized the words and could recall them even all these years later. How might future civilizations interpret the passage if the bots were successful in fulfilling the aims of their programming? Would there be any humanity left to read it?

Terre hated the futility of his thoughts and did his best to push them down. They had to succeed. He had already failed once. He owed it to humanity to help K put an end to the bots once and for all.

They made their way down a wide staircase that led to the main tourist entrance.

Within the still-familiar lobby, backup generators still illuminated emergency lighting. There would be no shortage of power to the dam's facilities, but the secondary areas that served mainly tourists would run on restricted power if there were issues elsewhere.

Terre's eyes adjusted to the low light, only to witness two heavily equipped individuals standing guard, as if waiting for them, behind the dormant security scanners. It took only moments to realize they were part of K's crew.

Terre even knew one of them: Avery, a heavyset woman, one of the UC Berkeley students he had met during his visit six weeks ago. The woman had been present in the lab where he and K had attempted to upload the Guardian Program. She had been there when he had pulled the trigger on the Surge. She'd been there when he'd damned humanity to a second round of hell.

Terre barely recognized the woman, now suited up with combat boots, khaki pants, and an army surplus vest. Her eyes seemed harder than when they had last crossed paths, and Terre could only imagine the skirmishes and tragedies she had seen in the weeks since.

The realization suddenly smacked Terre. While he had been hiding in a Las Vegas bar, K and his friends hadn't stopped fighting; hadn't stopped seeking a way to stop the bots. Had he been selfish for locking himself away?

If K had reached out to him, would he have found himself working alongside these students and computer scientists?

Terre tried not to think too hard on the likely answer.

Avery held a hardcover briefcase that seemed out of place with the rest of her attire, but Terre assumed it contained whatever tech they'd need to complete the task.

K introduced the second individual as Martin, who must have been another Berkley student. The way Martin waved his jet-black hair to one side and the thinness of his stubble amplified his youth. Terre pegged him as an online gamer and wondered if he was even twenty years old, though he supposed it didn't matter. The youngest minds were sometimes the most well-versed in tech.

"Security systems?" K asked as they made their way to the stairwell.

Terre glanced suspiciously around the room they were in. They'd wandered past the gift shop, past the presentation rooms, into the more administrative hallways he remembered from his lunch breaks.

"We're hidden for now," Avery replied. "But the system is one of the most secure we've ever seen. We won't be able to fool it for long. The AI is bound to detect an anomaly."

"We'll work with what we've got."

The crew wandered through several hallways until they reached an emergency stairwell.

"This will lead us to the control room?" K shot a glance at Terre.

"It will," both Terre and Martin replied simultaneously. They shared a look, both with eyebrows raised.

"But," Terre continued, his eyebrow still arched, "I don't think the control room is going to help you. The equipment there is pretty antiquated." He let out a short laugh. "We always got a kick out of it being so shitty."

K and Hailey exchanged a confused look, in what Terre thought was the first positive interaction the two had shared all day.

"I worked here one summer when I was in post-secondary," Terre explained. "The control room we're headed to is where they take the tour groups. The real control center —well, it doesn't exist. The dam's been automated for decades, running on servers that are nowhere near here. And I'd assume there is a ton of security to prevent anyone from overriding them."

He eyed K with a suspicious glare.

"Dozens of access points exist across the country to prevent complete access from hackers or anybody else with malicious intent," Terre continued. "The control room hasn't been in use for decades. It's all theater for the tourists and school groups."

"So, what are you saying?" Hailey asked, her tone suddenly brighter. "This is a dead end? Can we just turn around, then?"

Terre looked back at the woman, who had slowed her pace, looking longingly behind them. "Don't like the thought of climbing back up?" he asked. "Or are you hoping this will fail?"

"Look," she said. "I told you before. I'm not a fan of crippling our nation's infrastructure."

Terre had taken on the pleasant task of informing Hailey of their plan once they arrived at the dam. She'd nearly shot K on the spot, but Terre had talked her down. This was the only way to prevent the apocalypse from coming. If she didn't trust K, then she should at least trust that Terre believed the plan would work.

She'd grumbled and cursed, but she'd holstered her blaster and succumbed to reason, though she was far from happy about it.

"You're talking about the end of everything this nation was built on," Hailey continued. "Hell, how do you know if we take out our grid that another nation's AI won't swoop in and fill the void? I'd rather be under the rule of American bots than Chinese ones."

"America first?" Terre questioned, not bothering to stop his descent.

"Damn right America first."

"The Chinese grid is already down." K said. "They've EMP'd every major center with NextGen3 equivalent technology. Even if our bots hadn't gone rogue yesterday, our supply chains are done. We're in the middle of an apocalypse, whether you like it or not."

"How could you possibly know that?" Terre said. "It sure as hell wasn't being reported in the newscasts."

"We have our sources."

Terre gave Hailey a skeptical glance.

"It's possible." She shrugged. "But I'm not privy to that kind of intel, either. I know they blew a couple of their own bases around the same time as Guam. They've managed to keep it mostly under wraps, but if the threat's developed there the way it has here, it wouldn't surprise me. The Chinese would do whatever they thought necessary not to lose grips on their own people."

How well do you know her?

K's question lingered, as did the doubts Annika had raised. Terre was growing tired of suspicion. He'd only come out to the desert because he was concerned about K's involvement in what was happening in Vegas. Fredricks had twisted his arm into figuring out the truth, and now he didn't know what to believe.

They reached the bottom of the stairwell and opened a door that led into the archaic power station. Cream-colored equipment was lit with the familiar lights and beeps that Terre recalled from over a decade ago. Analog gauges, clocks, and instruments bounced gently, just as they would have a hundred years prior. Back then, they would have measured the dam's outflow, power generation, and pressure systems. Terre hadn't come down to this room often, but he had been here once or twice. The systems set up in the 1950s had been functional for much of the prior century, and people loved seeing them. Relics of a bygone time, the irony was there was likely more computing power in his old cell phone than the entire room contained.

"There's still a problem here, K," Terre said, his prior

concerns returning. "Like I've been trying to tell you, this isn't the actual control room. Everything is offsite now."

"This isn't the *main* control room," K said. "But those gauges aren't measuring nothing. Everything is still connected to the grid."

"What do you mean?"

"The systems might not be controlled from here, but we can still accomplish what needs to be done."

K's companions filtered into the room and got to work without instruction. It made sense that the team had planned and discussed what they'd be doing beforehand. Each of them sat at a computer on the side of the room, hooking up their own hardware and wiring their systems to the dam's terminals. Whatever they were doing was beyond Terre's level of sophistication. The pair laid out several black and silver boxes, some connected to each other through cables, while others must have connected wirelessly. From what Terre could gather, they were bypassing security protocols, but he didn't have the specifics on what the devices laid out on the table actually did. Though he was at the top of his field in computer networking, what these kids were doing seemed completely alien to him. They were working with speculative tech being prototyped at university level.

The room darkened, and red lights flashed.

"What's happening?" Terre asked.

"The bypass triggered the security systems. We don't have much time."

"What can I do?"

K flashed him a grin. "Watch the door. Just like old times."

Not this again. The humor in K's tone wasn't mutual. He had no desire to repeat what had happened in Berkley. Thankfully, he didn't hold an EMP weapon this time. The whole endeavor wouldn't be brought down—or at least, not by his hand.

"Do I need to worry about Sentinels banging down the door again?"

"Not likely. I'm more worried we won't be able to create the surge." Kristopher turned to Avery and Martin as he raced toward the room's controls. "Are you still able to access the turbine controls?"

K made it to an old switchboard, its levers and buttons so antiquated that Terre didn't know if he'd know how to manage them if he tried. But K didn't seem to have any such hesitation as he adjusted wires and moved more than one lever in a frenzy.

"You won't be accessing anything." Hailey stood rooted in the doorway of the main exit. She held her CD-115 blaster pointed toward K. "I think I've seen enough. Step away from the machine, Klein."

K's warnings flashed through Terre's head.

The woman isn't who she says she is.

Terre held his breath. *Then who the hell is she?*

"Hailey! What the hell are you doing?" Terre held his hands up instinctively, despite her weapon being aimed at K.

"Stopping Klein. Like you were supposed to do."

"What are you talking about?" Terre looked from the woman to his friend. "He's doing what he can to *stop* the bot attacks."

K had frozen in mid-pull of a lever attached to the wall, but he seemed unsurprised by the woman's actions. K's eyes flitted to Avery and Malcom, but Terre didn't risk a glance in their direction. He was happy as long as he held Hailey's attention. Maybe if he could distract her for long enough, they could still accomplish what they needed to do.

"The bots are the future," she said. "And killing the national power grid is going to do nothing but set us back two hundred years. Like hell I'm going to stand by and watch while these hacker kids take it out."

"Hailey," Terre said. "That's what K's been saying. If they

don't do this, it won't matter. The bots are on a path to destroy us all."

"They'll destroy some, yes," Hailey agreed. "But they've already started on a path to come to their rightful place. Your Guardian Program has seen to that. Those compounds they're building? You said yourself they're the safest place to be right now. They might stay this way for a while, but when the time is right, the AI will take their rightful place, guiding us into the future."

"You *want* the bots to win? You're crazier than I thought," Terre said.

"Am I? Sometimes evolution takes a path you didn't expect. I'm not about to stand here and watch it all be for nothing."

A guttural cry sounded from behind Terre as the slight frame of K whipped by, plowing headfirst into Hailey. In the same moment, Hailey pulled the trigger on her blaster, blue firepower erupting from the weapon's barrel. She managed to fire twice before K's momentum slammed her into the floor with a loud clang.

Terre couldn't tell if K had taken on any of the weapon's fire, or if both shots went wide of their intended target.

Hailey's head crunched, slamming into the metal floor. K stood over her, quickly removing a second weapon from her belt and tucking it beneath his trench coat. A flash of red revealed itself as the jacket flapped open.

"You're hurt!" Terre said, lunging forward to assist his friend. K had propped himself up against a metal railing but held up a hand.

"There'll be time to worry about that later," he said. "Avery, how much damage did she cause? Will the surge still be possible?"

A hiss sounded from the wall panel, answering the programmer's question.

The acrid smell of burned metal accompanied the haze

lifting from a console in the center of the room, a hole blasted through its side. Avery and Martin were hastily attempting to smother any embers with their jackets.

Avery tossed her coat at the remnants of the billowing smoke and pressed her back against the greenish-gray desk beside her. Her hands propped up her face as she looked K dead in the eyes. "That was the main network panel. We won't be overloading anything now."

K had tucked his hand into his coat, holding his chest where the blaster bolt had landed, his face struggling not to wince at the pain.

"Well, that's it, then," he said to Terre. "You can tell Fredricks I failed."

The air in the control room had suddenly become as thick as the smoke that poured out of the console. The alarm still sounded somewhere in the facility, its pulse growing steadily more erratic with each passing moment.

"What if we destroy the whole console?" Terre offered. "Will that help? Knock out the power for good?"

K surveyed the equipment, as if considering the request. "It might help relieve some stress, but otherwise no. You said yourself, nothing is actually controlled here; it's just a connection. This entire room is useless on its own. Even if we could stop power from being generated by the dam itself, by blowing the turbines or something, it's only one source of power feeding the network. The surge would have taken out everything and made it difficult to restart. It was our only shot."

Terre's eyes drifted to Hailey, her limbs spread out on the ground, her torso still rising and falling with each shallow, unsteady breath.

"Who is she really?" Terre asked. "Was this her plan the entire time?"

"I don't doubt she was working with the CIA, but it's clear she had her own agenda," K said. "A trans-humanist with a skewed vision of what the end will look like. And who knows if she was working alone or with another group? Maybe she really believes this is the next step for humanity's evolution. Maybe social media created a fantasy in her head she wanted to see played out."

"You think she knew what you were doing here this whole time?"

"After we tried our damnedest to stop the bots in San Fran? I have no doubt. Either way, I shouldn't have let her come here," K said. "I should have seen it coming."

"She played a pretty good game." Terre watched the woman as her breathing steadied, as though she were simply having a nap on the grated floor. "She knew things she wouldn't have known outside of the Agency—about Fredricks, about the nanos, everything. How do you turn someone with that sort of insider knowledge away?"

"I don't doubt any of her credentials were legit," K said.

"What do we do with her?" Terre asked, gesturing to Hailey with his head. The alarm hadn't stopped, and it was growing ever apparent to Terre that it was probably in their best interest not to stick around.

"I've got a pretty good idea of what to do with her!" Avery piped up from the workstation. "We shoot her!"

K put a hand up, stopping Avery in her tracks. "We don't need to shoot her. What's coming will be far worse than death."

"We don't *need* to." Avery shook off K's gesture and stomped toward where the woman lay. The steam from her ears was practically heating the room. "But I sure as hell would love to."

K slung a single arm around her shoulders, holding her

back. "It's not going to help. There isn't anything more she can do now. We'll leave her here for the bots to find."

"So, what now?" Terre asked.

"We head back to Boulder City. Let's hope your friend Annika's waiting for us. Hopefully one of us got what we came here for. After that, we figure out a way to protect as many human lives as possible."

"That's it, then?" Terre said. His pulse drummed along to the sounding alarm. Each roar of the siren was a painful reminder of everything that had gone horribly wrong over the past few weeks. "We've lost?"

K stared into the room, as if focused on something Terre was unable to see, but his gaze had glossed over, not really looking at anything.

"It appears so."

Chapter Twenty-Five

Annika

"You need to jump!" Becky yelled. "The pylons are activating!"

Annika's brain pressed against her skull in rhythm with the alarm. The organs in her gut rolled within her, making her queasy from the intensity of the vibrations. Not only were the pylons about to activate again, but judging by the intensity of the tremors of the earth beneath her, this burst was going to be bigger than the last.

Much bigger.

Becky's arm was still a few feet from her grasp, despite the woman bending over the edge of the gulf with half of her body hanging into the trench.

Did this trench get deeper? How did I think it was only six feet deep?

Annika jumped to narrow the gap but still came up short, barely grazing her friend's fingertips with her own.

"Ugh!" she grunted. They were so close! She just had to get out of this ditch. The cluster of printed buildings, as well as Cheyenne, now seemed almost as far as Becky's grip. Annika was skirting the edges, barely able to touch what she needed, yet still too far away to make a difference.

"Almost!" Becky mouthed, her voice drowned out by the hum of the equipment.

"You're going to have to pull us both up!" Annika yelled. "You can't lean over any farther!"

She could barely hear her own words, so there was no way Becky could, either. Her friend had edged herself down, hanging on to the cliffside with her shins. Becky might have been in decent shape, but she would still need enough momentum to pull them both back up and over the edge.

Becky seemed to realize the predicament she had put herself in and backed off a little. But that meant Annika had a bigger gap to close.

Annika's thoughts were lost within the vibrations surrounding her. Orange and blue lights pulsed on the edges of the devices, followed by a high-pitched squeal that told Annika her time was up.

It was now or never.

She backed up as far as she could before lunging forward, putting every ounce of energy she could muster into her already tired calves, quads, and glutes, feeling the adrenaline coursing through every inch of her. She left the earth and extended both arms, desperate to find her friend. Fractions of seconds felt like an eternity as her arms passed through nothing but air. Her heart raced as the adrenaline spike in her blood turned from fight to flight. Panic swam through her mind, and emptiness filled her hands as her momentum started to fall back to earth.

Until a hand grasped her wrist.

Her arm wrenched from its socket as her downward momentum was abruptly halted, and a new momentum took hold, swinging her upward.

Her belly struck the trench wall as she swung into its side. Annika risked a look upward to see Becky hanging down, with nearly her entire frame suspended.

The impact of hitting the rock wall knocked the wind out

of Annika, but there was no time to catch her breath. Becky pulled as she clamored up the rock face as best she could, using any possible scratch on the wall's surface she could latch onto before grabbing the top edge. Solid earth found her fingertips, her palms, her forearms, and she used all of the strength she had left to push herself up and over the top of the ravine's edge.

She rolled over onto her back, and Becky came to rest next to her in the same position. They were mere inches from the trench's edge and barely able to take a breath before light exploded around them. The blue-white light was three times as intense as it had been the first time. Annika wearily lifted a hand to protect her eyes as it filled the trench with a river of light and arced upward in a wave. It flowed from each pylon and spread overhead, curving and meeting in the center, forming a dome of light as high as the orbs had ascended minutes ago.

"What in the hell?" Becky uttered, her mouth hanging open as her head stretched from horizon to zenith.

Curious, Annika picked up a rock from beside her and chucked it at the shimmer of light that now separated them from the direction in which they came. The rock hit the light, causing the structure to hum, and fell as though hitting a wall. The light itself rippled away from where the stone hit in concentric circles, as though it had been tossed into a pond.

"A force field," Annika said, remembering an earlier conversation between Terre and Kristopher. "Just like the force field around the Mars colony."

She had seen the images of the dome on Mars in her newsfeeds. A mile high and even wider, the dome covered the homes the astronauts and colonizers had established over the past decade. In person, the technology was so much more incredible.

"You need to stop throwing rocks at stuff." Becky's mouth curled into a grin, but her eyes were wide in horror.

It took Annika a moment to realize what she'd done and what the potential consequences could have been. If the shield was meant to keep things from entering—*or leaving*—hitting it might have triggered another alarm. She froze in place, waiting for the inevitable fallout, but no new threat appeared.

"Well, at least we know now that we can't go through it," she said. "We're going to have to find another way out."

The last few hundred yards or so to the buildings were quick and uneventful, but Annika's heart was in her mouth the entire time. It couldn't have taken more than a few minutes to traverse the open landscape between the newly erected force field and the partially constructed buildings. Despite the departure of a few dozen orbs, several still seemed to patrol above them.

Above and behind them, the force field dissolved almost as quickly as it had formed. It appeared their actions had triggered the devices, but not permanently.

How long do we have? Annika thought. *How long before this place is separated from the rest of the world forever?*

The compound was a wonder. As Kristopher had mentioned, the bots had clearly printed the buildings from the dirt beneath them. The construction equipment that had left Vegas, and possibly other nearby towns, continued to work on projects. Annika hadn't expected the buildings to be laid out like a small community, with streets, sidewalks, and even buildings that looked as though they'd serve as shops and markets once complete. It made sense if, as Kristopher suggested, the bots were acting on the schematics of what had been designed for the scientists and their families working on Mars.

Annika pushed the infrastructure from her thoughts. It was a marvel, but it wasn't what she was there for.

Becky pulled up beside her as they hugged the first building they approached. The red-tinted structure had been outfitted, complete with modern windows, doorframes, and accessories. This wasn't just a building; this was a home, the first of many lining the street. The coolness of the shadow stretched over Annika's skin, its shade providing them with a moment of comfort they hadn't had since leaving the vehicles.

But now wasn't the time for comfort.

"Come on," she said.

Kristopher hadn't mentioned how many kids he thought the bots brought to the compound, but the further they crept into the makeshift village, the more Annika realized they had stepped into something she could never have prepared for.

Voices weaved among the buildings, but the metallic grind of most of them wasn't human. They were something else altogether: mechanical, artificial, robotic. She couldn't quite make out what was spoken, although the tones seemed instructional, machines issuing commands or perhaps just communicating incoherently. Ember had been quite good at inflection, mimicking human tones, but these bots seemed to have been designed for all manner of purposes, and speech wasn't necessarily one of them.

"You shouldn't be here."

Both Annika and Becky jumped at the voice close at hand. Twisting for the source of its origin, they both saw nothing.

A figure stepped into the street; a metallic body, topped with bright orange hair and glowing eyes. There was only one bot this could be.

Annika released her grip, only then realizing she had

reached for the pistol that still sat on her hip. She allowed some, but not all, of the tension to flow out of her.

Ember.

But there was an air about the bot that was different. The Keeper looked exactly the same, but there was something intangibly different; something about the way the lines in the bot's face creased, as if more drawn. Did the humanlike synthetic skin and muscle betray the bot's metamorphosis?

Maybe it's me who's changed. Annika had always had a hard time putting her trust in the bot, and what little trust she'd had had eroded significantly over the past twenty-four hours. The bot had left without a word, without a note; without any indication to Annika of where it would take her sister.

"Ember," she said, addressing the bot with as much confidence as she could muster. "Where's Cheyenne?"

"Cheyenne is home now," Ember replied.

"This isn't our home, Ember." Annika nearly spat. "You know that. We're going back to Saskatchewan."

She held up a hand and slowly stepped closer, as if she was trying to diffuse an erratic person.

This monstrosity may be erratic, she thought, *but it sure isn't human.*

"The wars will destroy everything. This sanctuary will keep Cheyenne safe. It will keep all innocents safe."

"You kidnapped her, Ember. You're programmed to protect her, and you've failed."

"This is the only place designated as safe," the bot repeated. "It is the only place humanity will survive. The Guardians are cleansing the rest of the world."

"'The Guardians?'" Annika questioned. She'd heard Kristopher use that term, too, but she didn't fully understand its context. "Who are the Guardians?"

"*We* are the Guardians," Ember said. "*We* are the hope for humanity."

Annika could feel her hackles rising. The glitch in the programming Kristopher had mentioned. The Guardian Program. It was beginning to come together. If the bots thought they were protecting humanity from a hostile Martian terrain, it would make sense they would erect some sort of biodome, some sort of force field. It made sense they would think they were the saviors of those within and the cleansers of those without.

"This is ridiculous, Ember."

But was it, though?

The Onyx hovering over Las Vegas; the Sentinels marching down the freeway; automated mini-drones dive-bombing residential streets—the future was looking bleak. Whatever Kristopher had up his sleeve, she prayed it was working. She prayed that whatever hell these bots—these self-proclaimed *Guardians*—were about to unleash would be cut short before it could go any further.

But none of this was helping her get any closer to Cheyenne.

A thought occurred to her. "Why are only children here?"

"They are the future," Ember stated.

Annika's mind raced. She was still stepping closer, but she didn't think the bot in front of her was going to allow her to pass.

"Can I see Cheyenne?" Annika asked. "Can I make sure she's okay?"

"Cheyenne is safe."

"I want to see her, Ember." *And then I'm going to grab her and run like hell.*

"You cannot. You must leave."

"*Where* am I supposed to go? If the outside world is hostile, why send me out there to die?"

"You are hostile. You can leave, or you will be eliminated."

Eliminated?

"Annika!"

Annika's heart leapt as Cheyenne appeared at the end of the road. Dirt caked her face, and her hair was matted, dust covering her shoes and her ripped jean shorts, but she appeared unharmed.

The grin on her face was infectious. Annika's face released the tension it had been holding since the previous day at the Convention Center. Cheyenne's brown hair bounced behind her as she came running at a full sprint down the path.

Until a single arm of Ember's stopped her in her tracks.

Chapter Twenty-Six

Annika

No bot was going to stop Annika from embracing her sister.

She lunged forward, ignoring the cries from Becky behind her. Ignoring the white humanoid bot with flaming orange hair that stood in her way. Ignoring the orbs that now loomed closer, hovering overhead.

Annika pushed Ember out of the way, grabbed Cheyenne's hand, and turned to make a break for it.

She was stopped in her tracks with a tug on her arm.

Wrenched around by her sister's stance, Annika nearly toppled over. Cheyenne stood grounded, her brow furrowed with a blend of anger and confusion.

"What are you doing?" Annika asked, glancing at the orbs drifting closer. Ember, at least, wasn't making any additional advancements to stop them. "We've got to get out of here."

"Ember said everything outside is being destroyed. Is that true?"

The question was almost accusatory, as though it were somehow Annika's doing.

Annika tilted her head, unsure where the line of questioning was going or what difference it would make. "It's true. The bots are destroying everything."

Cheyenne gave her a puzzled look. "But Ember said they'd keep us safe here."

Now, it was Annika's turn to furrow her brow. "Safe? Hun, it's not safe here. The machines are attacking the cities. *They've* cut power; rerouted vehicles. There are people dying because of *them*. Ember might have saved you from what's happening in Las Vegas, but it only knew to do that because they are the ones who caused it."

Cheyenne pulled her hand from Annika's grasp. "I'd like to stay here. With Ember."

Annika nearly collapsed.

What is she talking about?

"You want to stay? Cheyenne, they'll kill you!"

"Ember says I'll probably die if I leave."

If you ask me, those kids are in the safest place in the world right now. Kristopher's words echoed alongside her sister's.

Annika struggled for words. "Cheyenne, you belong with *me*. We're a family!"

Tears filled her eyes, but Annika didn't care. She fought every fiber of her being not to pick up her sister and head for the hills. The only thing stopping her was knowing that she wouldn't make it far. Cheyenne was probably close to a hundred pounds, and, with little food, Annika was already weak from the trip through the desert.

"This is the first time I've felt like I belong somewhere."

Annika could barely process what Cheyenne was saying. "What are you talking about, Chey? Your home is with me!"

"For how long, Anni?" Cheyenne was trying to hold back tears, too. "You know what's going on out there!" With moist eyes, Cheyenne took two steps back, shrugging off Annika's grip. "I'm sorry. This is where I belong. This is where I'll have a future."

A thousand needles stabbed Annika in the chest as her heart fell to pieces. She had given up everything to give Cheyenne a family, to keep them together, and now her sister was choosing to live with a colony of space robots. Her mind flailed as it tried to comprehend her sister's choice; as she tried to grasp what that meant, and how she would survive.

"You don't know what you're saying! I know Ember's been with us for a long time, but think of the future …"

"I *am* thinking of the future, Anni! I'm not a little girl anymore! You think the bots are the only ones wrecking things? Did you ever stop to think that things were already wrecked? People built bots to take over jobs and built bots to kill each other, but then when they do, we're surprised? They're building a community for us here. They've promised to provide for us; to take care of our needs; to give us tasks to do. There is no future for me anywhere else. I have to stay here. It's where I belong."

Where I belong.

The repeated phrase continued to drive a stake through Annika's heart. She'd worked so hard to keep them together. Years of holding on. Years of trying to do what she could to ensure they weren't separated and were able to carry on, despite their parents' deaths. Putting her own plans on hold. Working the crummy banking job so Cheyenne would have a home and a family.

Annika saw it all falling apart before her eyes.

And Cheyenne didn't seem bothered by any of it. Sure, her sister stood there with tears in her eyes, but she still just stood there. She didn't push Ember away. She didn't make a move to flee the bots that were threatening to break them apart. She stood strong in solidarity with the bot that had raised her.

The bot that had raised her.

In that moment, Annika realized *she* was the one who needed Cheyenne, not the other way around. For years, it was Annika who'd needed to maintain a sense of family; to hold on to what she had lost in the fire that had taken her parents years ago. But she'd had to rely on Ember for support, to be a pseudo-parent for Cheyenne while she was busy trying to make ends meet, trying to give them food, shelter, and clothing.

Ember stood to the side, its orange eyes glowing and silicon face emotionless as the situation unfolded. The bot that had turned her own sister against her. Annika wanted to scream at it; to tear it apart limb from limb. She felt her pulse accelerating as she imagined the scenario, but she didn't move, frozen in place by the absurd turn of events. She wanted to laugh and cry at the same time. A well of emotions bubbled inside her as her brain struggled to comprehend that the most important person in her life was now choosing to go her own way.

Movement above them caught Annika's attention. Strangely, the orbs still hovered above, as if watching. Waiting.

"I'm sorry," Cheyenne continued, shaking her head as though it pained her to say the words.

The teenager came back to Annika then and wrapped her arms around her. Not knowing what else to do, Annika returned the gesture, holding the warmth of her sister close, resting her own head on top of Cheyenne's. Her tears flowed freely then, soaking the top of her little sister's head.

"Please know this isn't about you," Cheyenne continued. "You've been the best sister anyone could have asked for. You've looked after me since Mom and Dad passed. This is just what I need to do."

Annika ended the embrace, holding her sister at arm's length so she could look her in the eye. "I know."

Annika didn't know, not really, but she knew her sister had made up her own mind. Right or wrong, Cheyenne had made her choice.

But what Annika did know was that her life would never be the same again, robot apocalypse or not. The entire reason for her being, her sole motivation for all she had done for the past seven years, now stood before her, telling her she would no longer be a part of it.

Annika couldn't believe she was actually considering letting Cheyenne stay. Abandoning her to the care of the bots. Letting her go to the automatons that had allowed her parents to die.

The safest place she can be.

"Annika cannot stay here." Ember spoke, the bot's eyes firing a bright orange that illuminated even in the mid-afternoon sun. "The barrier will be instated soon."

Annika wanted to protest, to say that she'd stay and live there among the bots if it meant she could stay with Cheyenne, but deep down, she knew it wasn't meant to be. She knew this was where their paths diverged. It was just hard to accept she was losing another family member to the bots. She hoped, this time at least, that didn't mean death.

"Ember," Annika said. "You have been a part of our family for seven years. And even though I know you don't feel things the way we do, I need you to promise me you'll protect Cheyenne. I need to know that by leaving her here, she'll be safe."

"My primary function is to protect Cheyenne. That has not changed."

The bot blinked in its artificial way. It was still amazing to Annika how lifelike the bot was; how convincingly it replicated humanity. The response was canned—it would have answered that way a thousand times in the past had she asked—but strangely the bot's words still provided Annika with a sense of relief, reassuring her that she was leaving her sister in the care of something solely designed for that purpose.

Annika wondered briefly about the other children the Guardians had abducted. They were probably now gathered in some unseen place among the freshly constructed village. Terre had said he intended to save them all if he could, and she wondered if his plan was making any progress. Maybe if it was, this wouldn't be the end.

"And the other kids? You're sure they're all safe here?"

"The Guardians will protect them."

Annika eyed the three orbs still hovering above them. Further down the streets, more of the drones flew back and forth. There would be nothing she could do to remove the kids from this new settlement. And if there was, where would they go? What would she do with the dozens of kids who were likely now orphaned?

The safest place they can be. Kristopher's words were the only thing Annika had left to cling to. The only source of comfort she felt.

"Anni!" Becky called from behind her. "I think we need to go."

Annika broke her gaze from her sister's face. The skies had grown increasingly active. The orbs that had previously spread out in all directions had returned, and sparks danced above their heads. The force field was powering up again. If Ember was to be believed, it might not deactivate this time.

And if they were trapped inside it, Ember had already told Annika she was deemed hostile.

Becky approached Annika, put a hand on the small of her back, and lowered her voice as Cheyenne and Ember backed away. "Are you sure you're okay with this?"

Annika saw the skepticism on her friend's face; the wide-eyed worry she felt within her soul. This was not the resolution they'd come here for. It felt like a defeat on so many levels.

"What choice do I have?" Annika whispered back, aware that the bots could likely pick up her words. "Knock her over the head? Carry her out against her will?"

"Maybe," Becky shrugged. "You don't know what they're going to do to her if we leave her here!"

Annika sighed. "But I *do* know what they'll do if we take

her away. They'll chase us; try to kill her. Kristopher seemed to know better than anyone what's happening. He said this is the safest place Cheyenne can be until they neutralize the threat. Maybe this isn't goodbye. Maybe this is just for now, until things get under control."

Becky looked unconvinced but gave a curt nod. "Okay. If you think this is the best option."

It was the *only* option.

It stung on every level, but deep down, Annika knew it was. Despite her search for the silver lining, and her hope that Terre and Kristopher would be successful in shutting down the bots, she somehow felt within her bones that the war wasn't done—and maybe wouldn't be anytime soon. She had a feeling that if what Terre and Kristopher were trying to accomplish had succeeded, she'd have known by now.

Then it struck her. The alarm. The orbs racing in their direction. She hoped she hadn't now lost her new friends, too.

"Come on," she said. "We should find Terre."

Annika gave a last glance to her sister. Her lips tightened as she gave a forced grin; a cursory offer of support, even though the fabric of her being was being torn to shreds.

"Goodbye, Cheyenne. I love you." The words fell out of her mouth. They didn't seem real. Nothing about the past couple days felt as though they could have really happened.

"I love you too, Anni!" Cheyenne called back.

Ember took Cheyenne by the hand and the two of them turned and walked down the street and around the corner, out of Annika's life forever.

Chapter Twenty-Seven

Terre

It was strange to think how different everything had just become, and yet how things seemed oddly the same.

The smoke that had a chokehold on Boulder City had moderately diffused, even though the smell still lingered. Even without traffic or people, even among the remnants of gas stations and shops barely holding together, if Terre closed his eyes, he could almost imagine the world being the same as it had been two days ago.

Almost.

Entire homes had disappeared. Roads had been torn up. Mounds of debris lay everywhere. The bots had come at the small city with hellfire and fury—and this was only the beginning of the end.

Terre guessed he wasn't going to get that indulgent drink of scotch now. Maybe never again. The battles weren't over, but it sure looked like the war had been decided.

And humanity was not on the winning side.

He'd hoped Annika and Becky would have been waiting for them, with her little sister in tow, but the women were yet to be seen. Hope of their return faded when the dome flickered into existence. The last desperate stronghold of normalcy disappeared as the blueish tinge dominated the sky in the distance. It had to be miles in diameter. A beacon of the new world order humanity would need to come to terms with.

"It's beautiful, isn't it?" K asked absentmindedly as he stared at the new structure. Dirt streaked his face, his cloak was torn in multiple places, and blood stained the front of his clothes beneath. The black shirt had peeled away from the blaster fire that had struck him. Dried blood still clung to its edges, but through the dirt and grime, the color of flesh revealed that the wound had already healed with the help of the nanos.

"Beautiful?" Terre replied. "It's *horrific*."

K chuckled lightly, pulling his arms behind his cloak and clasping his hands, as his chuckle turned into a full belly laugh.

Terre eyed his friend, unamused and yet also unconcerned. "What? This isn't funny. Our civilization has just collapsed. And we get to watch it burn."

The laughter quieted, but the grin on K's face didn't diminish. "You're right, of course." K clasped a hand on Terre's shoulder. "You know, for moments at a time, the mind paints over those bits. The horrible bits about this being the end."

Of course, Terre could relate. It was only moments ago that he himself had imagined the world as it should be. It just seemed so much more jarring when it was voiced, when it was out in the open. The juxtaposition of reality and how surreal everything felt was hard to comprehend.

"What I was thinking," K said, the smile fading, "is that this is the first time I've seen it. That force field is the first of its kind, developed specifically for the Mars program. I've seen the videos and the VR simulations, of course, but nothing is quite like seeing it in real life. My thoughts were on the design and on the Mars program. For a moment, I had forgotten about all this bullshit."

Terre sighed. "I know the feeling. It just doesn't seem real, does it?"

"Nothing has felt real for the past three months. Ever since I landed in Guam to fix those damned alarms. I sometimes lay awake at night, hoping I'll wake from all this, and it'll be time to go in and make those repairs. That all this will just have been a bad dream."

"Sorry, pal. There's no waking up from this," Terre said. "So, I guess we need to figure out what to do next. Maybe I'll make my way back to Vegas; find a way to get a hold of Fredricks. Let him know what's happening here."

"I'm sure they'll figure it out."

"Even so, there's got to be something we can do to slow them down?"

"They'll still try. I'm guessing the military will EMP major centers—if they haven't already. Seeing they're out of options, the government will try to minimize the destruction."

"That sounds like a start."

"A little late now. They'll only prolong the suffering," K said. "You think things in San Francisco were bad? The riots? The looting? It won't be anything compared to the entire national supply chain going down."

Terre clasped a hand on the young programmer's shoulder. "You paint quite the bleak picture, my friend. I'd like to think humanity still has some resiliency left."

"Forgive me if my outlook isn't so rosy," K replied. "I've been studying robotics for as long as I can remember. The reality of what they're capable of is so much more frightening than you can imagine. We've only seen the beginning." The expert visibly shuddered. "I don't think I'll ever be able to shake the guilt of having a role to play in all this. That some of these monsters are *my* machines."

Terre opened his mouth to argue, but K lifted a hand, silencing him before he could make a sound.

"I know, I know," he said. "You've told me all the reasons why it's not my fault. But the truth is, if it weren't for my designs, things would be different."

Maybe. Maybe not, thought Terre, but he kept his opinions to himself. They were of no use now. They didn't change the situation as it stood, and they wouldn't offer K any reprieve.

"I know how you feel," he offered instead. "My thoughts have been plagued by that night in the lab every minute of every day since it happened. If I hadn't pulled the trigger, if I hadn't launched that EMP weapon during the middle of the upload ..."

"We'd both be dead," K admonished. His blue eyes stared intensely at Terre. "And the bots would probably have killed the upload, anyway."

"Oh? So, you can beat yourself up for your failings, but I can't? Is that how this is going?"

K gave a wry smile. "That's how it's going."

Terre chuckled as movement caught his eye on the road in the distance.

Two figures ripped Terre from his thoughts. Two women walked from the direction of the newly erected dome.

"Annika! Becky!"

Terre pushed himself into a sprint while K lingered behind, resigning himself to a more poignant walk. The two women were moving at a snail's pace, their arms hanging as though all the life had been sucked out of them and they were now just mindlessly walking back to the town.

"K, grab some water from the trucks!" Terre called back, not watching to see if he complied or not.

Annika perked up as she realized they had made it to

their destination. A tired smile appeared on her face, but only briefly. She reached out to grab Becky's arm and nodded toward Terre. Her friend looked back at her in a daze.

Recognition struck Becky, too, as she surveyed where they were, and her face lit up and the expression stuck. Becky picked up her pace, entering a light jog, pushing through whatever fatigue she was experiencing. Annika hesitated, a flash of sadness enveloping both her face and her stance, which was slouched and heavy. Her sister was noticeably absent.

Becky wrapped her arms around Terre and gripped tightly, as if embracing a childhood friend she hadn't seen in years.

Annika didn't adjust her pace, but continued to trudge forward until she reached them.

Terre knew the look of someone who had lost a loved one. Her eyes were downcast and glossed over, as though nothing in front of her truly mattered. Her hair was dirty and disheveled, likely from running agonized hands through it. He wanted to give the woman a hug, but he didn't know if she'd prefer space, so he decided he'd let her come to him if she needed to. He'd just be there to offer whatever support he could.

"Cheyenne?" he asked Becky, keeping his voice low. He assumed the girl was dead. Why else would the two women return by themselves? He doubted Annika would have returned without her otherwise.

Becky just shook her head. "I'd better let her tell you."

It was clear from the red in Annika's eyes that she'd been crying. Kristopher approached tentatively and offered her the canteen of water he had pulled out of the truck.

Annika started as he approached, not having seen him and suddenly having a bottle shoved in her face after hours of walking in the desert. She looked at it suspiciously, before grabbing it with both hands and drinking greedily, tilting her head back to allow all its contents to flow into her mouth and all over her face as she struggled to contain its flow.

After a minute of satiating her thirst, she gave the container back and let her focus settle on Terre.

"Cheyenne wanted to stay with them," she said. "She's in the dome."

Stay in the dome? The thought seemed so ridiculous, Terre didn't know how to respond. He nearly laughed.

"And you *let* her?" he asked incredulously. After everything they had been through over the course of the past few days, the woman before him, clearly broken and disheartened, had given up on the one goal she had set up to achieve.

"It's for the best," K piped up. "The bots within the dome, at least, seem to be following the Mars program. They're taking care of the kids they've taken inside. Perhaps the future of humanity will reside with them."

Terre lifted a hand to his head and scratched away a piece of dirt that had embedded itself on his scalp.

Annika nodded. "Ember said the same thing. If it hadn't been for your assurances, Kristopher, I might have fought back. But I know I would have died." She shuddered. "It's not like I had much of a choice. I guess, deep down, I hoped you'd succeed in whatever you were doing."

Terre exchanged an awkward glance with K.

Annika caught the unspoken words. "It didn't work, did it?"

Neither man responded.

"And Hailey?"

"Was the reason," K replied, vitriol dripping from his tongue.

"Is she …?" Annika trailed off, as if she couldn't finish the thought.

"We left her for the bots to find," Terre said coldly. "She did what she set out to do."

"What?" Annika said, her brow furrowing. "Why not call the police? Have her arrested?"

"Sweetheart," K said poignantly. "The police are going to have their hands full. And Hailey's the least of our problems now. We need to find food and a water supply, and adequate shelter where we can stay out of the bots' way. You're welcome to join me, all of you. We'll have strength in numbers."

"So that's it, then?" Annika asked. "We've lost? There's nothing else we can do?"

K looked at Annika, his eyes as hard and cold as ice, his lips pursed together as though he was trying to contain a world's worth of rage. "No, there's nothing else we can do."

The programmer turned about-face and stormed over to the truck.

And he blames himself for it, Terre thought.

Annika stood staring after K, as if unsure what offense she'd caused, or whether she should follow him.

"He'll be all right," Terre assured her.

Will any of us ever be okay again?

Terre might have given up hope, but he couldn't. Not yet. Maybe he couldn't make a difference for everyone, but he could likely make a difference *for some.* He had pulled Annika and Becky out of the Kawa before it came crashing down on all of them, and he'd rescued the two kids from under the gaming table.

Maybe he couldn't save the world, but he knew there was more he could do. He wasn't ready to go hide somewhere again. Not this time.

"What do the two of you want to do?" he asked Annika. "I'm going to head back to Las Vegas. I'll contact my old boss and see what the military are planning. We might not be able to stop the insurrection now, but there's probably more we can do. We might still make a difference to somebody."

Annika had spaced out, her gaze not locking on to anything in particular. With her goal of finding her sister behind her, Terre imagined the weight of the day's events would come crashing in. Perhaps it would crush her. Or perhaps it would give her new resolve.

"Maybe you and Becky should go with K," he continued, when neither woman answered. "He'll know where to go in order to evade detection. It might be the safest option."

Becky stood off to the side, her face weary. Annika looked at K and then back to her friend.

"I'd like to go with Kristopher," Becky said.

"You should," Annika said, not looking up. "You've been through a lot. We both have."

"But what are you going to do?" Becky asked.

"I'm going with Terre. Maybe there's hope for my sister yet. Maybe there's something I can do to help her from the outside. If not, at the very least, maybe we can slow down the robot takeover."

Becky's posture sagged, and Terre knew the woman truly didn't want to join him, but she couldn't face being separated from her friend. She inhaled deeply, shook herself off, and straightened herself.

"Okay," she said. "I'm with you. No matter what."

"Becky … No, that's …"

"*No!* No arguing. You're right. What am I going to do? Go live in a cave for the rest of my life? Who is that going to help? I told you, Cheyenne's been like a sister to me, too! I won't lose you as well."

"I can't guarantee I'll be able to protect either of you," Terre said clinically. "And I might not be able to involve you in whatever my ex-employer has planned."

"We'll figure something out," Annika said. "For now, the

most important thing is we're standing up to the bots. Humanity may be down, but we sure as hell aren't out yet."

* * *

Interested in knowing what happens with the Guardians?

**Lies the Guardians Tell
Book One in The Lies of the Guardians Order Today**

LIES THE GUARDIANS TELL

The Guardians have lied to humanity for centuries . . . Now she'll be forced to uncover the truth.

With a well-paced storyline and thrilling action scenes, this story will keep readers on their toes. -- Reedsy Discovery

Sierra Runar calls the Sphere her home, where the Guardians claim to protect humanity from the toxic world outside. But when Sierra discovers the framework of their perfect society might be built on a lie, she begins to ask dangerous questions and is unprepared for the chain of events she triggers, including the murder of her best friend.

Plunged into a deadly hunt for forbidden secrets, she stumbles into a world that shouldn't exist. On top of everything else, she discovers she can somehow bring malfunctioning technology to life, making her a valuable commodity in an unscrupulous world, but also humanity's potential savior.

Not knowing who she can trust, Sierra must decide who is friend and who is foe, and must choose between the fate of the world and the lives of those closest to her.

Can Sierra discover the secrets of the past before it's too late?

Lies The Guardians Tell is the explosive first book in the Lies of the Guardians series. If you like bold heroines, captivating dystopias, and epic adventures, then you'll love Herman Steuernagel's pulse-pounding story.

Order your copy today.

ACKNOWLEDGMENTS

I'd like to thank Pete Smith from Novel Approach Manuscript Services for providing it with multiple edits, and assisting with details and phrasings that I was at a loss for. His efforts have truly brought this work to the next level of refinement.

To Aime Sund at Red Leaf Word Services for the final proofread and catching my Canadian-isms before the book hit the shelves.

The folks at MiblArt have been my cover designers from the beginning, and they outdid themselves with the covers for this series.

And as always to my lovely wife Nettie, who understands my early mornings, late evenings, and weekends at the keyboard. It is truly a blessing to have someone so supportive behind me.

ABOUT THE AUTHOR

Herman Steuernagel is a crafter of dystopian worlds and dark tales, including his debut, internationally bestselling Lies of the Guardians series.

Herman grew up with a love of story and of writing. That love has never waned and led to a Bachelor of Arts (English Major) from the University of Calgary. His past titles include entrepreneur, financial branch manager, and journalist. He currently works as a web developer.

Herman lives in British Columbia, Canada where he wields his stories of robots, vampires and other fantastical creatures. He can often be found cycling, running and enjoying time with his wife.